ELLIE ENGLE
SAVES ~~THE WORLD~~
HERSELF!

ELLIE ENGLE

SAVES ~~THE WORLD~~

HERSELF!

LEAH JOHNSON

SCHOLASTIC

Published in the UK by Scholastic, 2023
1 London Bridge, London, SE1 9BG
Scholastic Ireland, 89E Lagan Road, Dublin Industrial Estate, Glasnevin, Dublin,
D11 HP5F

SCHOLASTIC and associated logos are trademarks and/or
registered trademarks of Scholastic Inc.

Text © Leah Johnson, 2023
Illustrations by Natália Dias de Casado Lima © Scholastic, 2023

The right of Leah Johnson to be identified
as the author of this work has been asserted by
them under the Copyright, Designs and Patents Act 1988.

ISBN 978 0702 31346 2

A CIP catalogue record for this book is available from the British Library.

Printed by CPI Group (UK) Ltd, Croydon, CR0 4YY
Paper made from wood grown in sustainable forests and other controlled sources.

1 3 5 7 9 10 8 6 4 2

www.scholastic.co.uk

For the kid who needed a hero so badly that they became one.
For the kid who's still clutching their cape, too afraid to put it on.
This book is for you.

A hero isn't the one who always wins.
It's the one who always tries.

—Miles Morales

If you want to be a hero

first you need a great origin story.

Wonder Woman is from an island of women warriors who rule with fairness and fierceness—and to top it all off, she's the daughter of a Greek god. Green Lantern got his powers from an alien who saw that his heart was so pure that he'd never use them for evil instead of good. Black Panther inherited his abilities from a long line of supers, a family of rulers in the most technologically advanced country in the world. Whether you're a hero at birth or become one later in life, one thing is for certain: You gotta be extraordinary.

But real life isn't anything like comic books, because nothing in this town is extraordinary. Especially not me.

"New comic?" Abby hikes her duffel bag higher on her shoulder and falls into step next to me. I always meet her at her gym after Sunday-morning gymnastic practices. One, because I love hanging out with my best friend. But two, because it's not like I have anything else to do.

My mom is working, like she does most weekends, and the house was too quiet and empty for me. So I grabbed a couple of my comic books and headed down to the Rising Phoenix Gymnastics Center to sit on the bench out front and wait for Abby to get done doing the impossible flips and tricks that sent her crashing into me in the first place.

We met in kindergarten, at recess. The Ortegas had just moved in next door, but we'd never spoken. And Abby and I weren't in the same class, so I'd never seen her before. Then one day she was showing off on the playground, trying to remind everyone that she is the kind of nature-defying human that you can barely believe exists until you see her flying through the air. She overdid it on her back tuck, and I underdid it on my attempt to move out of the way. We've been stuck together ever since.

"Yeah, the new *Nubia*," I say now, looking down at the cover with a smile. I love all comic books, but *Nubia* is special. There aren't many heroes out there who look like me, and definitely not ones who have more strength than freaking Superman. I slip it into my backpack so I don't mess it up with my sweaty fingers. "You want to go to the pool today? Last chance before you-know-what."

"Ugh, I can't. Mommy is taking me to get my nails done. You know how she is—wants to do some back-to-school bonding or whatever." Abby's wearing a pair of jean shorts over her leotard, which makes her brown legs look longer than they are. She starts fiddling with her slicked-back bun until her dark brown hair hangs around her shoulders. "Sleepover tonight, though?"

"Obviously."

I try not to smile too hard at the thought of our annual back-to-school sleepover. I have some nervous flutters about starting at a new school tomorrow, for sure, but I can't even focus on that right now. All I can focus on is knowing that I'll get to stay up giggling and complaining and talking about schedules with Abby. We haven't gotten to spend as much time together since her training schedule picked up this summer, and I miss it. I miss her.

"Obviously." She does a bad imitation of my voice, and I laugh. "Well, okay, Captain Obvious. Oh my god, I almost forgot! You'll never believe what Bethany Thomas did today."

She goes on and on about her rival from her team landing a trick Abby can't do yet, and I half pay attention to her, and half look at everybody around us.

We walk past the familiar strip of businesses on Main. I

wave at Mr. Walker, who's sweeping the sidewalk in front of his bakery, Patty's Cakes, wearing winter gloves like he always does even though it's summer. Miss French is trying (and failing) to get her mean dog, Goon, to do a trick in the fenced-in dog park next door for the five hundredth time in as many days. Maisie and Marley Keilor are posing and taking pictures against the white brick wall beside the wedding-dress boutique to post on Instagram, part of their endless campaign to become twinfluencers.

We went to sleepaway camp with Maisie and Marley last year, and all four of us shared a bunk, so I know them. But they only say, "Hi, Abby!" in unison as we walk by, like I'm not even there. It used to bother me, people noticing Abby and not me, but not anymore. I like how calm it is in her shadow. There's no pressure to be and do anything except what I want to be and do. This is just how it is.

When things are predictable, my mom says, "I could set my watch by it." And I kind of do set my nonexistent watch by how reliable the people in this town and the things they do are. I like how much I can rely on this place to be overwhelmingly, exceedingly normal. It makes me feel less like a stranger in my own skin. Makes me feel less like there's something wrong with the fact that I'm just . . . what I am.

Unlike Abby, I like my life the way it is. Most of the time.

"I don't understand why I can't just, like, stop growing," she groans. She runs her hands over her sides and sighs. "Coach

Jillian says if I get much taller, I can pretty much kiss my dreams of vaulting in the Junior Nationals next year good-bye."

I want to tell her that she's pretty much perfect as she is. That she's crazy-powerful at any height, and unfairly beautiful, whether she's got crust in her eyes from just waking up or she's flying through the air in a bedazzled swimsuit. Nothing could change that, not even the extra inch and a half of height she picked up over the summer. But I keep my mouth shut. Abby wants Big Things from her life. And what Abby wants, she gets. I really love that about her.

Instead, I say, "If anyone could tell their body to stop growing, and their body actually listened, it would be you."

"Love you forever, bestie," she says, just like always.

I don't even have to think about my answer before it's coming out of my mouth, I've said it so many times. "Forever and two days."

She wraps an arm around my shoulder and smiles her huge smile, the one I usually only see when she sticks the landing on a dismount in competition. When I said I'm not extraordinary before, I guess I lied a little bit. When my best friend looks at me like that—like she only looks when she's doing the thing she loves most in the world—I can make myself believe I'm a little spectacular.

'Cause I'd have to be to earn that smile from Abby Ortega.

2

The inside of my head
isn't a bad place to be

which is probably why I spend so much time there.

I know that sounds weird, but whatever. According to Abby, I am a little weird. After all, what kind of twelve-year-old would rather read in her room than do, I don't know, anything else? I seem to be the only one at my school who does. Or, at least I was at our old school. Maybe things will be different at the junior high. I'm not holding my breath, though.

The thing is, I like my brain. Up there, I can dream up stories and symphonies and whatever else I want that doesn't exist in Plainsboro, Indiana.

Besides, Abby likes to talk. And she likes to show off. She likes to make bold outfit choices and Big Plans, and I think her bigness is enough for the both of us. As long as I get to be the first person she texts when she lands a new stunt in gymnastics, and who she spills her secrets to in passed notes during classes, and the one who gets to see her laugh so hard she snorts while watching Willa Moon movies, I feel big, too. Like her friendship makes me stronger just by association.

Back when my mom worked fewer hours and Abby came over to our house (because we had adult supervision—her mom is really strict about adult supervision), she used to say, "Abby has too much fire for her own good." I didn't really know what she meant, but it didn't matter much. Abby's fire has kept me warm for a long time, so it must be a good thing.

I think about what Abby must be planning to wear for the first day as I fold my outfit and put it in my small tote bag. I'll be in my usual: a T-shirt, jeans, and a big old cardigan in case it gets cold in the classroom. I slip my issue of *Nubia* into my backpack. My heart starts beating a little faster because I know it's almost time to see Abby again.

I walk downstairs and check the fridge for any notes from Mom. She could text me, but she likes the old-school way better. Her curly handwriting loops across the back of the envelope that's held on to the fridge with an old Yardley and Sons Heating and Cooling magnet.

Make sure to lock up and feed Burt. Don't forget to grab your lunchbox from the fridge. Love you, Belly Baby!

I take the paper and fold it before stuffing it in my back pocket. Ugh. My eyes feel hot all of a sudden like I'm about to cry, so I run my hands over my face as if I can scrub all the emotion off it. I know Mom works to take care of me and that's why she's gone so much. I know we never see each other *because* she loves me so much. I just have to remember that.

I love her, too, so I won't cry. I need to be strong so she can do what she needs to do without having to worry about me.

I sprinkle some fish food into Burt the Betta Fish's bowl on the counter and tell him good night as he swims to the surface to pick at the food I just dropped. I grab my lunchbox—the plain black one that my dad used to carry to work when he lived in Plainsboro—check my pocket for my keys and my phone, and leave my too-lonely house behind.

*

The Ortegas live next door, but it might as well be another world.

First of all, there are way more people here than at my house. It's honestly hard to keep track of everyone coming and going. There's Monty, Abby's big brother, who's gonna be a senior this year. He spends all his time listening to his music extra loud, trying to sneak his girlfriend into the house when Mr. and Mrs. Ortega aren't paying attention, and drawing pictures he won't let anyone see. And then there's Iz and Dani, her two little sisters, who love to play pranks on each other (and like it even more if the prank makes the other one cry). Last year, Abby's mom had a baby—Manny, who might be the cutest human being on the planet, even though his cries sound like a tornado siren and his diapers are disaster zones. And then there's Mr. and Mrs. Ortega, who are always cooking something delicious or making embarrassing puns (that I secretly love) or kissing like their lives depend on it.

It makes me sad sometimes how much their house reminds me of the way things used to be at mine, but mostly I'm just happy to be a part of it. Even when the sound of two pairs of feet thundering down the hallway outside Abby's bedroom for the hundredth time in the past five minutes is so loud, it rattles the walls a little.

"You two, I swear if you don't cut it out, I'm gonna scream!" Abby pokes her head out the door to yell at her sisters. Dani and Iz have been racing each other up and down the carpeted hallway over and over again, trying to decide who's the fastest between them. Sometimes Abby gets squashed in the sandwich of her brothers and sisters and all their commotion. Monty and his music, the twins and their pranks, the baby and his crying. I'm surprised Abby manages to keep her hair looking so good all the time, because I'm pretty sure I'd be pulling mine out. I love the Ortegas, but they're a lot to handle.

When the twins don't stop racing each other, Abby yells for her dad. "Daddy, can you please tell these two monsters to cut it out? Me and Ellie need our beauty rest for our first day tomorrow!"

I hear his voice in the hallway before I see him. When his face appears in the doorway, he's got a giggling Dani and Iz under each arm and that big smile he always has on his face.

"You don't need beauty rest, mami." He leans in and kisses Abby on her forehead. "You get any more beautiful, and I'm gonna have to start scaring boys away from our front yard."

Abby rolls her eyes, but I can tell she's happy. "Us girls can take care of ourselves, Daddy."

"Of course you can. But where's the fun in that for me?" He winks at both of us and laughs. "Night, you two. See you in the morning!"

When he leaves, Abby shuts the door and climbs back onto the bed with a sigh. The two of us sit cross-legged on her bedspread, facing each other. We only have about an hour before we need to go to sleep since we have to be up bright and early for school in the morning, so we're doing the same thing we've done for every back-to-school sleepover for the past six years: I'm half reading a comic book while pretending to understand anything Abby's saying about the celebrities she's freaking out over.

"Isn't she just *so* chic? I'm thinking about growing my hair out long. Like this." Abby points to a picture of Willa Moon on the cover of the most recent issue of *Teen Vogue*. Willa's hair is white-blond and reaches all the way down to her butt, even in the high ponytail she's wearing. "What do you think?"

"I think Willa Moon should start going by DeeDee the Detective again. That was her best work." I smirk.

Before Willa was a big-time pop star, she had a TV show where she played a kid detective who sang and danced to figure out the clues to her cases. It was weird, but I kind of liked it. When I was eight.

Now she's more famous than Jojo Siwa with more money than Taylor Swift. She even has a reality show about her life in Malibu with her two yippy little dogs, Monkey and Martian, which everyone—from my classmates to my poppy (well, before he died)—watches. It's pretty intense.

Abby loves the idea of being famous. She loves reading about the glamour and the attention (and especially all the drama). Her collection of glossy magazines is nearly as big as my collection of comic books. I guess I understand why she cares so much. I mean, the life of a world-famous celebrity feels like a dream—too shiny and perfect to be real. When I was younger, I thought about what it might be like to be a different kind of person, one who loved having the whole world know my name, who would think it was fun to go to fancy parties and dinners and hang out with beautiful, worldly people.

But I'm not cut out for that stuff. Not the parties or the

gowns or the paparazzi. Honestly, all that would probably make me wanna shrink down to the size of a meatball and roll myself out the door just like that old camp song. Besides, I always came back to the same thing, that my life was good as it is. That there was no world better than one where I get to live next door to the Ortegas, and dance in the living room with my mom, and go to Wrigley's to read comic books with my poppy.

And then my dad left, and Poppy passed away, and I thought about it again. All the time. Abby would flip through her magazines, and I'd look at the posed pictures of shiny, polished celebrities getting caught off guard by paparazzi, and wonder what it would be like to have all the money in the world. Not what it would be like to wear diamonds and super-pointy high heels, but to never have to worry about whether the coupons in the drawer were expired. Or if your mom was gonna have to work for twelve hours straight to pay the bills again. It felt like a fair trade: You might lose your privacy, but at least you could take care of the people you loved most in the world.

Abby reaches behind her, pulls out the puffy pillow she's lying on, and brings it down on my head with a soft *thunk*. She scrambles out of the bed to avoid my retaliation and giggles, "That's what you get for not having better opinions on my hairstyles!"

I dive after her with a pillow of my own, and now Iz and Dani aren't the only ones in the house causing a ruckus. I get a solid hit in with my pillow, and Abby holds a hand up to her forehead and pretends to swoon like a woman from one of those old black-and-white movies. Forget gymnastics; Abby should be an actress, she's so dramatic sometimes.

I kneel down next to her and pretend to take her seriously.

I put on my best old-timey accent. "My apologies, madame, is thy head with injury?"

"Please, you must leave me now as I perish!" She sits up long enough to grab my face in her hands, and then immediately falls back to the ground, her tongue lolling out of her mouth. She looks like a dead fish with slightly fewer scales. It's so funny, and so familiar, I laugh hard enough to snort.

Abby's eyes spring open at the sound of my cackle, and she uses my distraction to halfheartedly whop me back. Before I know it, we've traded enough whacks with our pillows while shout-laughing at each other's attacks that Mrs. Ortega has to peek into the room.

"It sounds like you two are in here stirring up trouble," she says.

Iz and Dani poke their little curly heads around her legs to see what's going on, so I twist my face into a silly expression to make them giggle.

"Get into bed before I send your father up here to embarrass you with his comedy routine," she threatens. "He's got some new puns about motor oil that I'm sure you'll just love."

"Ugh, *okay*, Mommy," Abby groans. She jumps up and extends a hand to help me stand.

Her mom gives us both a wink and a "Good night, my loves," before shutting the door behind her.

When we flop back on the bed to catch our breath, Abby smiles the way she only does when it's the two of us. So wide that I can see the one tooth on the side that grew in crooked and that she says makes her look bad. I like that she trusts me to see her at what she thinks is her worst, even though I know every version of her face is a really good one.

The only light in the room is her bedside lamp with the pink shade, so the whole room looks like a piece of candy. Something bright and sugary and almost too sweet to eat. I've always loved it. In the hallway, I can just barely make out the sound of doors shutting and water running as everyone gets ready for bed. The house creaks a little as everything starts to settle for the night. We both crawl under the comforter, and I practically melt into the mattress. Abby pulls the string on the lamp, and the whole room is suddenly shadows.

"Are you scared about tomorrow?" she asks after a moment of quiet.

Her voice is a low whisper, and for the first time in a long time, it sounds shy. It's easier, sometimes, in the dark, to say what you mean.

"What is there to be scared of?" I turn onto my side to face her. She has her hair in two French braids so it'll be wavy in the morning, and I reach out to tug on the end of one. "It's just school."

And we'll have each other, like always. Sure, we don't have most of our classes together for the first time ever—I'm taking Advanced Language Arts and Advanced Science, two classes that make up a pretty big chunk of the day—but we'll still meet up during passing periods and our shared lunch. It's not the best situation, but I'm choosing to look on the bright side: There's no better way to survive seventh grade than by complaining about greasy cafeteria pizza and soggy green beans with your best friend every day.

She presses her lips together like I'm not understanding.

"Yeah, but it's *junior high*. This is a big deal. We're not gonna be kids anymore, you know. We have to start acting more mature."

We've got a long time until we're not gonna be kids anymore, I think but don't say. Sometimes Abby's brain moves faster than our bodies. She's always so many steps ahead.

"I want to make my mark," Abby says. She turns to stare at the ceiling. "I don't want to get swallowed up."

I feel weird looking at her when she's not looking back, so I lie flat on my back, too. I don't answer for a long time. I don't care about making my mark. There's only one person's attention I want, and I already have it. It may not be exactly like my heart sometimes tells me it should be, but that's okay.

It isn't until her breathing evens out and I think she might be asleep that I whisper back.

"Nobody could forget you even if they tried."

3

We don't have earthquakes in Indiana

so even though everything in the room is rattling—framed snapshots from Abby's life falling from the walls, the antique jewelry box she got from her abuelita shaking off her dresser and crashing to the floor—my first thought is that the Apocalypse has finally come.

My poppy was really into Jesus, and nearly every day he told us that the Rapture was coming soon. We used to call Poppy cuckoo, but maybe the old man was onto something. It's gotta be the end of the world as we know it, and I'm freaking out.

I shoot up in bed, and Abby does, too. Her eyes are wide

and her flyaways are going crazy and my heart is beating out of my chest. One of Abby's gymnastics tournament trophies falls to the carpet and snaps in half with a loud *crack!* I hear baby Manny crying in the hallway and the twins screaming. Abby wraps her arms around me, squeezes tight, and I wrap mine around her. I tuck my face into her shoulder and take a deep breath until her coconut shampoo is the only thing in my brain. If these are my last seconds on earth, I think now might be a good time to tell her the truth. That I think I might—

"Oh my god, what *was* that?" Abby screams the second the shaking stops.

I can't answer, though. Because as soon as everything stills, I suddenly feel like we're on top of a mountain. My ears pop and the air feels as thin as a sheet of paper, hard to get enough air into my lungs with each of my breaths. When I hold my hands out in front of me, they're shaking like autumn leaves. I force a deep breath in and let it out slowly, just like my old counselor used to tell me to do when I got too worked up about something. I close my eyes and press my palms against my eyelids as I try to come back down to earth.

Abby hops out of bed and flings open the door, but I feel frozen to the spot, buried underneath her pink comforter. It takes a few more of those big breaths before I feel steady enough to get out of bed. When I finally throw the covers off my legs and run to the door, my voice even feels shaky.

"Did you feel that?" I ask.

"Of course I did!" Abby cocks her head to the side. "I bet everyone in Indiana felt that earthquake."

"No, I mean, afterward," I say, looking down at my hands again. They're not shaking as much anymore, but my body still feels all wobbly. "Everything felt like . . ."

I try to find a comparison, but all I can come up with are moments from comics that I know Abby wouldn't understand. Abby's entire family is in the hallway in their pajamas, looking scared. Except for Monty. He's yawning and shaking out his shaggy black hair and dragging himself to the bathroom like this is just another day. Mrs. Ortega rushes out of the nursery with Manny in her arms, cooing at him to help him calm down. Mr. Ortega walks down the hall and runs a hand over everyone's heads like he's taking inventory. Ears, eyes, noses, mouths, all still in place.

So . . . *not* the end of the world, then.

"You know in *Infinity War* right before the Avengers got blipped?" I whisper to Abby.

She watched all the Avengers movies with me because she thought Captain America was cute, and she even cried when Thanos came through and snapped Peter Parker into dust. I'm hoping she understands what I mean, because in the instant after the earthquake, I felt like my body didn't belong to me for a second.

"It was like that. Super-weird."

I open and close my fists a few times and make note of every tiny detail, but nothing about them has changed. Chipped blue polish from our last girls' night manicure session, a brown birthmark on my left thumb, and a small scar on one of my knuckles from falling off my bike in the first grade are still the only thing worth paying attention to.

"I only felt the earthquake." Abby shakes her head. She presses a hand against my forehead like she's taking my temperature. "Maybe you're sick?"

I'm not sick. Or at least I don't think I am.

My heart is rattling like a train about to run off the tracks. My entire body feels like it's full of the fizzy lifting drink from *Willy Wonka and the Chocolate Factory*. Even the hairs on my arms are standing up. I can't believe my seventh-grade year started off like this. The world shaking itself awake was bad enough. But I almost told Abby the truth. I almost ruined everything.

"Is everyone all right?" Mr. Ortega asks as Dani runs to press herself against his side.

"Ay, dios mío. An earthquake," Mrs. Ortega says. Her hair is piled on top of her head in a big messy bun, and some curls fall out as she bounces Manny on her hip. "I could have sworn we left those behind in California."

I stand behind Abby and look around her bedroom. Aside from some crooked pictures, a broken trophy, and the jewelry box on the floor with Abby's necklaces spilling out of it, everything looks the same. My ears feel too open, like when they pop right after a yawn, only times a million. And my fingers are tingling a little, but I figure that's just a leftover from getting popcorn-popped awake this morning.

"I'm going to turn on the news and see what just happened." Mr. Ortega checks the clock on the wall and clicks his tongue. It's a little after 6:30, which means we have to be at school in an hour. Ugh. "You two might as well start getting ready for the day."

Abby talks nonstop as she starts to shake off the scare from this morning.

"I wonder if me and Marley are gonna have any classes together! Isn't she cool?"

"When do you think cheerleading tryouts will be? I've gotta make the team."

"If we have casserole for lunch today, I'm definitely gonna barf."

She's settling back into her usual fearless routine. But while she worries about cheerleading and lunch and Marley Keilor, I still feel like I'm buzzing.

Maybe it's because when we were clinging to each other in bed during the earthquake, something finally clicked. I knew exactly what I wanted to say to her, what I've wanted her to know but have been too scared to tell her for months now. That I don't feel the way she feels about boys. That I don't want them to look at me and call me cute and ask me out.

I want those things with *her*.

The room suddenly feels really small, and my heart is beating too fast. Monty knocks on the door on his way back to his room, his usual signal that the bathroom is free, and I grab my bag of clothes and dart in there without another word after he leaves it open. The mirror is still all steamy from his shower, and the humidity kind of chokes me as I stand there trying to catch my breath.

I feel like I just ran a marathon, like I'm *still* running a marathon. All the feelings from before, when I had trouble getting myself out of bed, hit me like a semitruck. It's been a long time since I've felt this way. It's worse than being nervous. It's like something in my throat is trying to claw its way out and like I'm breathing through a straw. I try to settle down by thinking simple thoughts. I start with what's in the room.

A toilet with the seat still up (because Monty is the worst). A small plant with fifteen leaves that are currently going all brittle and brown on the ends, in a tiny silver pot sitting on the counter next to the hand soap. I keep my eyes on the plant, and it makes me think of all the flowers Mrs. Ortega has killed in the six years they've lived here. She calls herself a black thumb instead of a green thumb, since everything she tries to grow dies.

I run a hand over the plant and try to focus on the way the leaves feel under my fingers, brittle and delicate. It takes a second, but eventually I'm calm enough to get dressed. I brush my teeth quickly and take off my bonnet to shake out my shoulder-length kinky twists. I trade my pajamas for my first-day outfit and look myself over in the mirror.

You look fine. Totally normal. Everything is okay.

Mr. Ortega knocks twice on the door, shaking me out of the stare-down I'm having with my reflection. He calls from the other side: "Any and all preteen girls who intend to start seventh grade this morning better shake their tail feathers if they want bacon before we leave!"

I take one more deep breath and pull open the door with a smile. Mr. Ortega is dressed in the blue jumpsuit he wears at his garage and claps his hands together once.

"Come on, Engle, we got places to be and people to see." He looks behind me. "I've been meaning to throw out that old plant, but— Huh. I guess it doesn't look too shabby today, does it?"

I turn, wondering if I missed a plant when I was trying to calm down a minute ago. But the only plant I see is the same one from earlier, but it looks way greener and less like it's knocking on death's door than it did when I was checking it out. Ugh. School hasn't even started yet and my brain is already fried.

"Must be that Ellie Engle charm, huh? Gives the whole room some pep." He squeezes my nose once just like he does to Abby's and strides down the stairs, calling more warnings as we go: "Monty, if you're late for first period, you can kiss that motorcycle good-bye!"

Abby rushes out of her room, hair and makeup done exactly like the pictures of her favorite celebrities that she has taped around her floor-length mirror. She looks like a Christmas gift that someone spent a ton of time wrapping.

"Well"—she hikes her backpack up on her shoulders and stops in front of me to do a spin—"how do I look?"

"Um . . . shiny?" I want to bang my head against the wall as soon as the words are out of my mouth, because that's really not what I meant to say, but it must have been good enough, because Abby beams.

"Yes, that's *exactly* what I wanted! I'm using the new Willa Moon highlighter stick to add glow to my cheeks, see?"

She waves a hand in front of her cheek, but I don't really know what I'm looking at. All I can think about is that the way my stomach feels all flippy definitely doesn't have to do with the earthquake anymore. I'm pretty sure my hands are shaking for a completely new reason.

Abby was right: Seventh grade *is* gonna be different. And I couldn't be less ready for it if I tried.

4

My body feels too big
for the cafeteria

and I'm too aware of everything.

It's been like this all day. I could hear Genesis Calloway grinding her teeth from three rows over during first period. I could smell Ty Collins's breath—some weirdly disgusting mix of spearmint and hot sauce—in second block even though he was on the other side of the room. And now, sitting at our table in the cafeteria, I can practically feel Abby's heartbeat in my own chest, it's so loud.

"So, then I said, 'No, did *your* boobs get bigger over the summer?' Can you believe she would ask me that? How rude can you— Ellie, are you listening to me?" Abby waves a hand in front of my face, and I shake my head like that'll knock loose the cobwebs in there.

The earthquake is all anyone has been talking about in any of my classes today. *It was the first of that magnitude in fifty years! The news said it was a freak occurrence! The windows at Patty's Cakes are completely shattered!*

I don't focus on any of it, though. I can't wait for this day to be over so I can go home, maybe take a nap, and wake up feeling like myself again.

"Yeah, you said Bethany objectified you in gym class." I try to smile, but my skin feels too tight on my face.

"*Objectified?* Oh my god, where do you even get these words? You're too smart." She drops her tray onto the table and bites a baby carrot between her front teeth with a too-loud *snap!* We sit across from each other, and she rests her head on a fist with a pout. "Bethany isn't even the worst part, though. No one has noticed my new glitter eyeliner *or* the fact that this is almost the exact same hairstyle Willa Moon had on her show last week! The earthquake is ruining everything."

I *hmm* so it sounds like I'm listening. I push my green beans around with my plastic fork. They smell all tinny like they just got dumped out of a can, and the scent is so overpowering, I can't imagine actually eating them.

"What's up with you today?" Abby asks. "You've been off since this morning."

I open my mouth to tell her the truth—that I had a panic

attack this morning. That I want to hold her hand in the hall-way. That everything is suddenly so *much* I can't even think straight. But instead, I say, "I think I need some sleep. The earthquake interrupted my REM."

Abby rolls her eyes with a smile. "Okay, Sleeping Beauty."

If only I actually was Sleeping Beauty, and all my prob-lems could be solved with a (kind of creepy, honestly) kiss, life would be easier. But this isn't a fantasy, this is real life. Which means— Wait.

Sleeping Beauty is all about a girl who's been cursed. Sure, the prince and the witch and the good fairies are the fun stuff to get little kids to pay attention to the movie, but if you take all that away, it's not that wild, right? It's just a story where some-one is struck by an unbelievable occurrence—okay, in her case, a mystical and magical one—beyond her control. *What if . . .*

My brain starts firing on all cylinders, pulling together all the weird stuff from today. I don't know how I didn't think of it sooner, but there must be something supernatural floating around like an airborne disease created by a Disney villain. I look around the cafeteria to see if anyone else is acting out of the ordinary, but the only strange thing I see is a boy from my gym class laughing so hard he snorts milk out of his nostrils, which I'm pretty sure is the opposite of magic: puberty.

Soon, two people we knew from elementary school sit at our table, which means Abby can tell her story about Bethany's rudeness during gym class all over again. I don't mind that

Abby is my only friend, but Abby loves having a big audience. It's one of the reasons she enjoys gymnastics so much, because every routine she does commands attention. Sometimes I don't like that, feeling like I'm not enough for her the way she is for me, but I'm happy about it this time if it means the attention is off me and how weird I feel.

I tune out Abby's voice and press the heels of my hands into my eyes. The combined smell of school fried chicken and soggy green beans is suddenly too much to take. I push away my tray and spend the rest of lunch trying my hardest to pretend like I can't hear the girl from my math class whispering secrets to her boyfriend at the table all the way over by the door.

*

I'm sure something is wrong with me by the time I get home from school. I can hear my mom mumbling inside the house and smell the chicken nuggets Mrs. Ortega is feeding the twins before I even pass our mailbox.

Abby is still at school, staying after for the cheerleading callout meeting, but I couldn't wait to bolt the minute the final bell rang. Riding the bus was awful. Too loud, too smelly, and too crowded. But it got me home faster than if I had walked, so it got the job done.

"Belly! Belly Baby, come in here, please." I practically run to my mom in the kitchen. I feel like a little kid, but I just want to hug her. I tuck myself up under her arm and hold her tight. Her heartbeat sounds like a jackhammer in my ear. "Oof. Oh wow. Hey, hon. I missed you, too."

I take a deep breath, and the smell of her usual lavender-scented perfume is almost overwhelming.

"I have bad news," she says.

I pull back just enough so I can look up at her face. It's round with big brown eyes like mine. Some people say we look so alike God must have just pressed copy and paste to get me.

"Belly, Burt . . ."

I turn to where Burt the Betta Fish's bowl is, and my breath leaves me. I know fish don't have long life spans. I read about it in our sixth-grade science textbook. But I didn't think I would have to say good-bye so soon.

I got Burt the Betta Fish two years ago, the day my dad moved out. My dad got a new job in Arizona, my mom got new divorce papers on her bed, and I got a new fish.

I'm pretty sure it was my parents' way of saying sorry, even though they had nothing to say sorry for. It wasn't their fault they didn't love each other anymore. It's not like they wished for it to happen or anything. I don't know, I think adults are just like that. Sometimes their guilt leaks out all over the place in the weirdest ways.

My house got quiet way before my dad moved out. First, they argued all the time. And then they just stopped. One day

I had parents who loved each other, the next I had parents who couldn't stand to be in the same room with each other, and then I had parents who pretended not to know each other. I know it really took years for them to decide they didn't want to be married anymore. But that's how life goes, I guess. It changes so slowly you barely even notice change is happening until it's over.

Dad left while I was at school because I guess he was worried I would freak out. I used to do that sometimes. When I was in kindergarten, I would cry so hard every time he dropped me off, I would slip into a panic attack before school breakfast. All the other kids would be eating their Pop-Tarts and drinking their juice, and I would be in the nurse's office. She'd always ask me to point out everything in the room one at a time.

Cabinet. Wheelchair. Desk. Band-Aids. Tissues.

And when I calmed down enough, she would send me to class.

It wasn't until I heard my mom at parent-teacher night that it clicked. I waited out in the hallway with my dad, and while he talked to Mr. Ortega, I leaned in to listen to her confide in my teacher.

"I just don't know what to do with her. She's not like this anywhere else." Mom hiccuped between sobs. "I worry all day at work that one day she's just not going to stop. That you all are going to call me and tell me I have to come get her because she's cried herself sick."

I stopped crying after that. I didn't want my mom to be afraid anymore.

I didn't cry again until the night after my dad left. While up in my room with the lights off, I thought about Burt the Betta Fish swimming around downstairs, the world's most oblivious good-bye gift, and I cried myself to sleep.

My mom never knew, though. I didn't want her to worry. She had enough on her mind by then without me adding to it.

Today, I look over at the glass bowl and realize my mom has covered it with a dish towel. The most pitiful memorial ever.

"What do we do?" I ask.

"We have to flush him, sweetie."

I'm not sure if fish get funerals. I've never done this before. Today has been a day full of terrible firsts. First time being woken up by an earthquake. First time almost telling my best friend that I might like her as more than a friend. First time feeling like a member of the Great Value X-Men brought to life with all these weird and unexplainable new sensations buzzing through my body. But before I can even start thinking about any of that stuff and what it means, I've gotta lay my good buddy, the best fish in the universe, to his eternal toilet rest.

I nod. "Okay. I'll take care of it."

"You sure?" She puts both her hands on my shoulders and holds me a little away from her. "I can help."

"No." I shake my head. I can handle it on my own. "I'll do it."

She looks down at his bowl and runs a hand over the top of the dish towel.

"You were a loyal fish, Burt," she says. "You swam like a champ up until the very end."

5

A fish funeral is a lot like a normal funeral

except people wear a lot less black. I'm wearing a pretty regular red Captain Marvel T-shirt and a pair of ratty old jeans with holes in the knees. I think Burt the Betta Fish would want things casual. He was laid-back like that.

I scoop Burt the Betta Fish out of the bowl and onto the towel. I walk to the bathroom to give him his last rites before sending him on to fishy heaven. I imagine it'll be something like *Finding Nemo*. I'll flush him, and he'll make it to his final resting place somewhere beautiful, like Wallaby Way, Sydney. I kneel in front of the toilet and try to come up with something to say.

I think of all the days I sat at the counter doing homework with no one but Burt the Betta Fish to keep me company. Mom at work, Abby at practice, Dad long gone. Burt the Betta Fish and his floppy little tail, swishing back and forth and back and forth like it was the simplest thing in the world. Like I was perfect company, just me and my math homework and my silence.

And I know it's stupid, but then I get all emotional.

He was just a little fish, but he was *my* fish. He was mine to take care of and love, and now he's gone. I wonder if my dad even remembers that he gave him to me. Probably not. I haven't talked to him in a long time. He got engaged to some lady I don't know a few months ago, and I guess that's kept him pretty busy. Last time he called, he said he wanted me to fly out to meet her before their wedding, but he hasn't said anything about it since. It's like he forgot about the trip and then about me altogether.

"I'm sorry, buddy," I say, swallowing around the lump in my throat, because I have nothing else to offer.

I think of one of the prayers Poppy used to make me recite but change it a little to fit the occasion a little better. "Um, God in heaven, hear my prayer. Keep Burt the Betta Fish in Thy loving care."

I forget the rest pretty quickly.

So instead of a prayer, I recite memories. Like the time I tried to sneak him to school for show-and-tell, but the water from his bowl just ended up splashing all over the inside of my backpack, and I got caught before I even made it to the car. Or the time I was almost convinced he could understand me because he kept glug-glugging at the perfect points in a story I was telling him. And all those nights it was just the two of us—Burt the Betta Fish in his tiny, quiet home, and me in mine—in front of the TV waiting for Mom or Poppy to get back home.

I tell myself not to cry, even though the backs of my eyes start to prickle. I tell myself he's just a fish. But as I tilt the towel toward the toilet bowl and his little scales shine in the light, I know that's a lie. He's not just a fish. He's my friend. He's *family*. And I don't want to lose him.

I wipe my nose with the back of my free hand and say, "See you on the other side, buddy."

I wish I could smooth my fingers through his fur like I would if he were a cat or a dog, but since I can't, I run a finger over his scales one last time and—

"Thunderbolts of Jove!" I shout.

In one of the old comics, Wonder Woman yells "Thunderbolts of Jove!" before going into battle. I'm not sure what Jove is, or why she's calling for its thunder, but it feels fitting for a moment like this.

I fumble the towel with Burt the Betta Fish flopping on it and scramble across the floor until my back hits the wall. I can hear Burt land in the water with a little splash, and I shut my eyes tight and shake my head. There's no way. There's just no way. It's impossible.

I try to take a few deep breaths before opening my eyes. Burt the Betta Fish was most certainly dead as a doornail. And even if he wasn't dead when he was floating at the top of the bowl, the amount of time he was outside of water on top of that towel would have been enough to do it.

I crawl forward, and my heart feels like it stops beating in my chest. Maybe I'm losing it. Maybe I'm a supervillain. Plenty of their origin stories begin with a slow slide into insanity. Like Harley Quinn! Yeah, that's gotta be it. I peek over the edge of the toilet seat and gasp.

There's Burt the Betta Fish just swimming around. Back and forth and back and forth like this isn't the most massive, colossal, monumental thing that's ever occurred in the history of humanity. Everything that's happened since this morning comes rushing back to me. The random earthquake. The plant in the Ortegas' bathroom. The ability to hear things from far away. There's no explaining this away.

My fish was dead two minutes ago.

And I just brought him back to life.

Comic books are fake

and that's okay. I learned early that Miles Morales doesn't need to be a real boy, swinging through the streets of New York City, for me to believe in him. The Flash doesn't have to use the Speed Force to sprint down Main Street for him to be a real-life hero. What superheroes mean to people—to me—is enough. Maybe when I was a younger, I thought that one day someone would swoop in and save everyone I loved from the scary stuff, but I've grown up since then, okay? I'm old enough to know the truth: There's no such thing as superheroes.

So how in the name of Kamala Khan did I just pull a fishy resurrection out of my back pocket?

"Oh no, oh no, oh no, no, no, no, no," I whisper as I scramble off the floor.

I dip the bowl into the toilet water to scoop out Burt the Betta Fish and don't even think about how many pee germs I'm splashing around the room in the process. Who has time to think about all the bacteria Mr. Meyer was always talking about during science last year when I've literally just defied the laws of nature? There's no time for hand sanitizer!

In every comic book, someone who can raise the dead is called a necromancer. Ugh, even the name of the power sounds intense. Why couldn't I have gotten something casual like X-ray vision or—or even telepathy? Telepathy is totally harmless!

"Belly, are you okay? You want me to come in there?" My mom's voice is muffled outside the door and that's when it hits me—I'm gonna have to go on the run. Yup, I'm about to go full X-Men, be banished to the Xavier Institute before I've even memorized my entire seventh-grade schedule. My mom can't handle a superkid living under her roof. She doesn't have the skill set!

I can already imagine the teary good-bye: *Oh, Belly Baby, I love you so much, but you must go be among your own kind!* And *boom!* No more Mom. No more Abby. No more quiet, perfect Plainsboro. I have to keep this a secret.

"Um, yes, yeah, I'm okay!" I look around the bathroom for a way to sneak Burt the Betta Fish out without being caught.

At least he's not a dog, I think—then I'd have to worry about his wayward barks giving me away. Oh my god, could I bring dogs back to life, too? No way. All this is impossible. I try to make my voice sound sad. "I just need a minute to"—what did my mom say all the time after Poppy died?—"mourn! I'm just mourning for a second!"

"Okay, honey. Call me if you need me."

I wait until I can hear her footsteps padding away from the door before I shove the fishbowl under my shirt, wrap my arms around my waist, and sprint upstairs. The toilety fish water splashes against my stomach when I rush inside my room and slam the door. I lean back against it and close my eyes. Just think, Ellie. WWND? (What Would Nubia Do?—my life's motto.)

She would problem solve. She would also probably crush something with her super-strength, but I figure we can do without breaking anything for now.

I open the bottom drawer of my dresser and pull out all my T-shirts until they're covering the floor. I slip Burt the Betta Fish out from under my shirt and rest his bowl inside my empty drawer.

"Sorry, buddy," I whisper. "I'll be back for you tonight."

I'll have to google if darkness is safe for fish later. Right now, I gotta plan.

Rogue could suck the life force out of someone with her bare hands, and that's kind of like what I just did with Burt the Betta Fish, only in reverse. So I think I have to cover mine just in case. I dive under my bed and dig out a pair of hot-pink sparkly mittens that Abby left in my room last winter and I never remembered to give back. After I pull them on, I crouch in front of my bookshelf and grab every comic book I can think of with a necromancer in it and shove them into my backpack as carefully as I can. I mean, I can't use most of my fingers at the moment, so not super carefully, but still.

Even though Abby is at cheerleading callouts right now, there's only one place I can think of going when my whole world has pretty much flipped upside down. So I shout my good-byes to my mom, take the stairs two at a time, and beeline to the Ortegas'.

*

There's nothing Abby hates more than surprises, so they're usually something I avoid altogether. Her parents tried to plan a surprise birthday party for her when we were in fourth grade. When she walked into the room where we all jumped out to say happy birthday, she was sweaty and still wearing her shorts and leo from gymnastics instead of a brand-new birthday dress and a hairstyle she'd spent an hour on in the mirror. So she immediately turned, walked out, and locked herself in the bathroom for an hour until everyone finally left.

None of us ever tried to pull one over on her again.

Which is why I guess I should have expected her to start screaming bloody murder the second I told her about my new powers.

The sound is even louder than usual now that my hearing has gone supersonic, so I squeeze my eyes shut like that will help block out the noise before jumping in front of her and slapping a fuzzy mitten over her mouth.

"AHHHH—" Even with my hand there, it takes her a second to stop screeching like a banshee. I shake my head so hard it feels like my brain just rattled loose. After the day I've had, I bet I could probably reattach it to my brain stem just by blinking my eyes twice and saying some magic words or something. Who knows what I'm capable of at this point!

When she stops, I take a step back just as Mrs. Ortega pops her head into the room. Manny is in her arms staring at his drool-covered chubby fist like it is the most mysterious thing in the universe. I've never wanted to have the problems of a baby more than right this second.

"You girls okay? I thought I heard something in here."

I widen my eyes and raise my eyebrows and try to silently tell Abby not to say anything. I don't think I can add telepathy to my list of abilities, but she presses her lips together for a second before saying, "No, Mommy. I just thought I saw a bug in here."

"I have told Monty over and over again that eating in his room attracts ants, and does he listen to me? No!" Mrs. Ortega throws her free hand up in frustration before backing out of the room. I can hear her yelling to Mr. Ortega downstairs to call the exterminator as she stomps down the hall. I lean back against one of the tall posts on Abby's bed and run the mittens over my face. That was such a close call.

One more misstep like that and it's the real-life Xavier Institute for sure.

"Abby—"

"No!" she shouts, before lowering her voice. She's still wearing her outfit from school, but her hair has gotten a little frizzier like it always does after being out of a ponytail for a long time. She tucks it back behind her ear before leaning forward to hold my shoulders at arm's length. "No way, Ellie. This is too much. You've just—you've been reading too many comic books, that's all."

Abby doesn't hate comic books or superheroes. She just doesn't care about them or understand why I do. She says the lessons in them are too cookie-cutter and the heroes are unrealistic. Which is why I'm not surprised when she blinks and adds, too seriously, "We *will* get you the therapy you need."

I shake her off and roll my eyes. Abby only even knows what a therapist is because of me. I saw one for a few months after my dad left, when my mom thought something might be wrong with me because I never got upset about him moving out. I was never happy about it, either. I just kind of went blank. At least in front of her. It was easier for everyone that way. And after six months, one appointment a week, she and the therapist mostly just gave up. As long as I kept doing my homework and eating my vegetables at dinner, I must have been fine.

I ate a *lot* of broccoli that year.

"Why would I make up something like this?" I hold my hands in the air and wave them around like that will explain everything. I'm starting to freak out. If she doesn't believe me, I don't know what I'll do. "It's too hot to be wearing these for no reason! It's August, Abby! Does anybody in Indiana wear mittens in August?"

"Mr. Walker does." She shrugs.

Oh, yeah.

"Okay, but Mr. Walker doesn't count. He's"—I think of what my dad used to call him a long time ago—"*eccentric*."

Mr. Walker owns Patty's Cakes, the bakery on Main, and he's my mom's boss. He's also kind of like my second grandpa, even though he's sort of strange. He's got gray hair that comes out of his ears, and friendly eyes, and one gold front tooth, which I used to think meant he was secretly a pirate. But he's always, *always* wearing gloves, no matter what season it is. Everyone thinks he's a little off his rocker, but I've always thought he was just a little … different. A good different. Like me.

"Yeah, but— Wait. Are those my mittens?"

She looks at me like she's seeing me for the first time since walking into her room fifteen minutes ago and finding me hunched over the laptop on her desk. I don't have a laptop, so I do all my computer work either at Abby's house or the library. Mrs. Ortega didn't even blink before letting me upstairs to wait for Abby to get done with cheerleading callouts. But seeing as how Abby has sort of flipped out on me, I almost wish I had come up with a better plan than just blurting out, *I can raise the dead!*

"And why is your shirt all wet?"

I forgot to change my toilety-water Captain Marvel shirt. Oops.

She shakes her head. "You know what? Never mind. I don't even want to know."

She flops down on her bed and plops a pillow over her face. For someone who didn't develop superhuman abilities overnight, she sure is taking this hard.

After a minute of silence, she pulls off the pillow and sits up. She looks determined, like she does when she's supposed to be mastering a new stunt in gymnastics.

"Okay, so Burt was dead?"

I nod and don't bother correcting her on his name. It's Burt the Betta Fish. You gotta say the whole thing or else it loses its zest. But whatever. Now clearly isn't the time.

"And you touched his scales, and he came back to life?"

I nod again. I swallow down the bubble of nerves rising from my belly. It sounds insane. I probably wouldn't believe it either unless I'd seen it with my own eyes.

"And you have no idea how this could have happened?"

I shake my head. If I knew, I'd be running to whatever

warlock or emissary who could reverse this instead of camping out in my best friend's bedroom, sweating through a pair of winter gloves in the tail end of summer.

Abby nods. She bites her lip and I look away for a second because my stomach always gets all funny and flippy when she does that, and now is really, seriously, absolutely not the time for that.

"All right, grab your comic books. I'll get Monty's laptop so we both have one."

She puts her hands on her hips, and I feel better already. It's me and Abby. Abby and me. We can figure this out. We've been able to get this far together. There's no way something as silly as world-changing, humanity-defying, life-giving powers could be what breaks us apart.

My fingers are buzzing, and from downstairs I hear Mr. Ortega drop a pan after pulling it out of the oven with his bare hands as clearly as if it's happening right in front of us. I'm trying my hardest not to freak out about it. Abby smooshes my cheeks in her hands like she's done since we were six, and I smile even though my face is pretty much Play-Doh right now.

"We got this," she says.

And because she's never steered me wrong before, I choose to believe her. Or, at least, I try to.

*

Supernatural homework can't be graded, but if it could, after an hour of researching, me and Abby would definitely be getting an F on the "How to Keep Ellie from Ripping a Hole through the Fabric of the Known Universe with Her Extensive and Inconceivable New Powers" assignment. I've been thumbing through comic books while Abby explores creepy websites that come up with some stories even wackier than mine, and we're no closer to figuring out what's wrong with me or how I got here.

"Were you drenched in a vat of radioactive fluid?"

"No, Abby."

"Did you get bitten by a radioactive spider?"

"No, Abby."

"Okay, how about—"

I turn around to give her the evilest eye I can. See? We need all of Jove's thunderbolts right about now.

"Let me stop you. If your next suggestion includes radioactive waste, paste, underwear, or arachnids, the answer is gonna be a big, supersized, *Still no, Abby.*"

I flop my head down onto the vintage Agents of S.H.I.E.L.D. comic book that I inherited from Poppy and groan.

"I told you, I woke up this way. I think it started this morning, with the plant in your bathroom," I say into the soft old paper. "After the—"

I sit up straight and look around. I have about twenty comic books spread around me on the floor, but unlike textbooks, comics aren't always designed to give you answers. Most of the time they just raise more questions. *How is that possible? Will the bad guys ever win? Could I be a superhero?* And up until this morning, I thought I knew everything you could know about superpowers—how you get them, who is worthy of them, what it takes to keep them. But I guess that's always how it goes. You don't know what you don't know until what you don't know is staring you right in the face.

I grab an issue of X-Men and flip through the pages. There are hundreds of stories about supers that get their powers by some random, unlucky thing happening to them and setting their entire lives on the path to good and evil or whatever. In this issue, Cyclops gets his powers after a plane crash, and I obviously wasn't on any plane. But there was an earthquake. Which is pretty boring on the list of ways to acquire superpowers, if I'm being honest, but it would explain everything starting from the moment I was woken up this morning.

I hold up the book in front of Abby's face.

"'The earthquake, Abby! It was the earthquake. Just like the plane crash for Cyclops or the car crash for Jessica Jones or— Wow, there are a lot of crashes in comic books, that's probably something to think about."

Abby throws her hands up. "Ellie, get to the point!"

"Oh yeah, what I'm saying is, this is typical origin story material: Something mysterious or wild happens and then just like that." I snap my fingers. "Chemicals get into your body, change your DNA, and leave you with the ability to fly. Or a trauma changes you so deeply, like, down-to-your-molecules deep, and gives you the ability to shoot beams out of your eyes. Or an earthquake happens and—"

I stop because Abby's eyes have bugged out and her eyebrows have reached her hairline, and I think if I say anything else about the comic book lore that might explain all this, she'll actually self-destruct. And I don't have time to reboot her today; there's already too much going on.

I take a deep breath and try to sound calmer than I feel.

"I don't know how, and I don't know why, but I'm almost a hundred percent sure that what happened to me started with the earthquake this morning. It's the only thing that makes sense." I lean back against the bed. "They said it was pretty much impossible to have that size earthquake here, right? And we still did."

The improbable meeting the impossible is pretty much the formula for every superhero origin story ever. And this is definitely improbable and impossible all rolled up into one Ellie Engle–sized mess.

"Well, okay, I guess that makes as much sense as any of this does." Abby jumps up off the bed when she sees me start collecting all my comic books from the floor. "Wait!" She grabs my shoulder and turns me around. "So how do we, you know, fix it? Because this is a disaster waiting to happen."

Fixing *it* means fixing *me*, and I have no idea what that

would look like. But I know I don't like the sound of it, even if these powers are the last thing I want to deal with right now. Abby likes things she can control, things she can understand. But these powers are way, *way* outside of what either of us understands. So I just shrug.

"I have no idea." I sigh. "But I think I need to get some sleep before I can even start figuring it out."

Mrs. Ortega yells up for dinner, and I decide to try again tomorrow. Maybe, if I'm lucky, I'll wake up in the morning and everything will be back to normal. Abby will be Abby, I'll be regular-degular old Ellie, and all will be right with the world. You know, besides the ice in the South Pole melting and all the puppies stuck in too-crowded animal shelters and stuff.

Abby walks me downstairs and cocks her head to the side before I walk out the door. I can tell she doesn't feel good about me leaving, not when everything feels so weird and we didn't come up with any answers. But I just can't sit down for dinner with the Ortegas and pretend everything is normal while Monty inhales his meal like a human vacuum, the twins try to one-up each other with how gross they can make their food look, and Mr. and Mrs. Ortega make kissy faces at each other across the table. Nothing is normal about this day, not even a little bit.

"You sure you don't want to stay for Little Italy night? Dad is making calzones."

Mr. Ortega is better at making Italian food than any

chef at an Italian restaurant I've ever been to. Better than the Olive Garden, even. So if I'm skipping Little Italy night at the Ortegas', it's gotta be serious. I shake my head no and Abby pulls me in for a hug.

"This is okay, El. We're gonna figure out how to get rid of this."

I don't know why, but the thought makes my chest get a little tight. This just became a part of me, and already we're trying to figure out how to lose it?

Instead of weighing any more of the pros and cons of joining the legions of the supernatural, I hug Abby back and yell good-bye to the whole family—but no one can hear me over the marching band–loud chaos that is the Ortegas at mealtime— and I drag myself next door.

It's dark and quiet when I walk back in the house. The only light comes from the quick flashes of color on the TV in the living room. In the kitchen, there's a pepperoni pizza that we've had in the freezer for two weeks on a cookie tray on top of the stove with a quarter of it missing. I grab a piece and take a bite out of it even though it's been sitting out for a while, and instantly wish I'd at least grabbed a calzone to go from next door. And then I think about how tired my mom must have been making dinner after working all day and I feel a stab of guilt.

Mom wakes up at four every morning to go to her job at Mr. Walker's bakery before heading to her afternoon job of tutoring high schoolers. She teaches them how to boost their college admission test scores so they can get into fancy schools, which is a big deal to some of the parents in Plainsboro, I guess. Back before Dad left, Mom used to work full-time at the bakery. Baking is her favorite thing in the world, and I think it helped that she got to work with Mr. Walker, one of the nicest guys ever. I practically grew up with flour in my hair and a sugar cookie in my mouth.

But she always says, "Baking cakes doesn't pay bills like helping rich kids cheat the system does," so she went down to part-time a while ago. She'd never say it, but I know she misses spending all day at the bakery so much some days it hurts.

I click off the TV and set the remote on the coffee table next to Mom's feet. I pull the quilt off the back of the couch and tuck it around her body. Her mouth is open a little and she's snoring quietly, so I push her chin up until she smacks her lips in her sleep. I can count more wrinkles around her eyes than I could a few months ago, and my heart feels like it's too big for my chest with how much I love her.

I close my eyes and focus on the sound of her heartbeat. *Buh-boom. Buh-boom. Buh-boom.* It's loud, so much louder now than it's supposed to be, but it helps me focus. She doesn't need any more stress. She doesn't need anything else to worry about. I think about what came of Uncle Ben in Spider-Man— how the people who love supers are always the ones who have to pay the highest price for their amazing powers—and I know I have to fix this *thing*. And I have to do it fast.

When I finally go to bed, it's that gentle rhythm in my mom's chest from an entire floor away that finally lulls me to sleep.

I've never been the class weirdo

but showing up to the second day of seventh grade in mittens and earmuffs in August is a pretty sure way of *becoming* the class weirdo. Which Abby makes sure to tell me the second I meet her at her locker. As soon as she sees me, she looks around quickly, grabs my hand, and pulls me around the corner into the dark and musty alcove behind the stairwell where no one can see us.

"Oh my *gawd*, Ellie, what are you wearing?" She sounds shockingly like Willa Moon on her reality show when one of her assistants does something especially embarrassing at her annual birthday extravaganza, like wearing white after Labor

Day or asking Taylor Swift how to spell her name for the guest list.

I roll my eyes. "What?" I pretend like my outfit—jeans and an old Stark Industries shirt my mom found in the boys' section at Target—is totally normal. Which it mostly is. You know, except for the mittens and muffs. "I think I look pretty good today."

Abby palms her forehead so hard I think we might have to call in the nurse for a concussion. As usual, she looks like she just left a photo shoot for some preppy clothing brand. Her brown hair is straightened and up in a high ponytail, and she's wearing a pair of gold sandals with a sleeveless light yellow romper with little red flowers all over it and a jean jacket so she doesn't get busted for violating dress code. I don't care about fashion as much as she does, but I've always loved how we kind of balance each other out. But I guess my new . . . *accessories* are a step too far.

"How are we supposed to make our mark when you—" She cuts herself off and shakes her head. I very patiently don't bother mentioning that I'm not the one worried about making my mark. "Look, can you at least lose the ear things? No one—and I do mean no one—is gonna sit near us at lunch if you show up looking like the Abominable Yeti."

"The Abominable *Snowman*," I correct her. I mumble, "If you're gonna insult my supersuit, you might as well get the name right."

I cross my arms over my chest. It's not like I wanted to wear these stupid things today. It's just . . . I needed something to help block out some of the noise so I would be able to pay attention in class. And I have no idea what my hands are capable of after what happened with Burt the Betta Fish, so I have to keep them covered until I figure it out. But Abby is making me feel like I have some sort of highly contagious illness and if she stands too close, she might catch it. Last time I checked, being a nerd wasn't transmittable.

"Whatever!" She throws her arms in the air like she's had just about enough of me. "Give me the—the things!"

She puts a hand on her hip and taps her foot until I drop the earmuffs in her hand. The bell rings for first block and I huff. I can't believe I wasted my entire passing period on this when there are actual crises to deal with—like the fact that there are no explanations for my entire life being screwed up with powers that I thought were impossible until twenty-four hours ago.

"I swear, Ellie-Welly, sometimes I feel like you were transported here from Mars." Abby smooshes my face a little harder than normal, shakes her head, and whispers, "No one can find out about this. If you become, like, some kind of circus act or something, we'll never live it down. No one will talk to us! And then we'll never make our marks."

Her eyebrows wrinkle up like they do whenever she gets super stressed.

I gulp. The way she says it makes it sound like she's the one who got stuck with these stupid powers and not me. And like word getting out would be the worst thing ever, not because it would flip my life upside down, pancake-style, but because it would keep us from being popular like Maisie and Marley Keilor. Abby's freaked-out expression makes me feel the same way drinking orange juice after brushing my teeth does: pretty much terrible.

She catches sight of Maisie and calls for her to wait up while she waves over her shoulder. And when she takes a step into the wave of people washing down the hallway to catch up with her, I try not to think about the fact that she didn't bother to say good-bye.

*

I'm glad to be surrounded by nerds when I finally plop down in my first day of Advanced Language Arts. Now that we're in junior high, we're on a "block schedule," which is just a fancy way of saying we do half our classes one day, and half our classes the next, split up in huge blocks of time. I don't know if I like it yet, but I definitely like not having to listen to Mr. Meyer, my old sixth-grade teacher, complain about cancel culture in between every subject.

Anyway, it's nice to be in a class full of people who care

about stuff like books and reading as much as I do. For a minute, it makes me feel less like the citizen of Mars that Abby apparently thinks I am. Until I really start looking closely at the people around me.

If I have superpowers, then that means anyone could have them. I don't know what the statistics are on something like that, but it only makes sense, right? Once, I googled "Is it normal to have a crush on your best friend?" and learned that one out of every five people says they may be something other than straight. There are a lot of different ways to feel about people, apparently. And knowing that made me feel a little better, a little less different.

This is just like that, only with fewer Google search results.

I pull out the pocket-sized notebook that I usually keep for passing notes with Abby and start collecting my data before the bell rings to start class. I dart my eyes back and forth, trying to be discreet, as I take in the scene. Mostly people are just finding their seats and talking, but there are a few suspects. My pencil scratches across my paper quickly as Julian Jacobs blinks six times in a row behind his thick Coke-bottle glasses before taking them off to clean them. But while he's cleaning them, he closes his eyes. Very suspicious.

✓ Closes eyes when they're uncovered.
✓ Very Scott Summers, but not as cool.
✓ Destructive optic beams? Will keep watch for further observation.

I'm deep in detective mode until the person behind me starts talking.

"Nice gloves."

I smile when I turn around and see who it is. I must have been too distracted by all my super-sense overload to notice her. Breonna Boyd looks pretty much the same as she did at the end of last year, only she has new, round wire glasses that remind me of Arthur the aardvark only cooler, and her already dark brown skin is even warmer and shinier because of the summer-vacation sun. As usual, though, her hair is pulled into the big, cloudlike puff on top of her head that always kind of reminds me of my mom's go-to pineapple-in-a-scarf style.

"Oh, Bree, hey!"

She gives me the tiniest little lip twitch because Bree never really smiles. If she had a superpower, being stoic would probably be it. Once, in second grade, a spider fell from the ceiling into Justin Murphy's shaggy red hair, and he screamed so loud the windows practically rattled while he danced around like someone had dropped an ice cube down his pants.

He ended up knocking over the class ant farm, our bean sprouts in the window, and our teacher's computer monitor. It was the funniest thing any of us had ever seen. We laughed so hard we cried, and then Carrie Bell peed her pants a little, which made us all laugh even harder.

Bree didn't even crack a smile. Didn't even look up from

her copy of *The Phantom Tollbooth*. That's when I knew she was her own type of invincible.

I've always thought she was cool, even if we're not really friends.

"I didn't know you were in this class," I say. I point at her beat-up copy of *The Book Thief*, which wasn't even on our summer reading list, and add, "But I should have guessed, huh? You read even more than me."

She looks down at her desk and shrugs, but I can tell she's happy I said it.

I don't even have to strain to hear the girls one row over whispering about us, clear as a bell. It's Marley Keilor and some girl I don't know, their voices low but just loud enough for me to hear.

"What's up with them? They're so like *that*, you know?" Marley says. "They must be from Davis."

The other makes a gagging noise before they both break into giggles.

Plainsboro is a small enough town that we only have four elementary schools that feed into two junior high schools that eventually become one big high school. Davis Elementary— where me, Abby, and Bree went—is on the side of town that's okay, but not super-nice. Like, most of the houses are a little bit older and a lot of the people rent instead of buy. I never knew what the big deal about that was, but Mom always made it seem like it was some huge thing. Like buying your house was a sign that you were really rich or something.

I never thought much about it until we were surrounded by kids from the other side of town in this school. They all have this *shine* to them. Like someone drew them by hand and erased every stray pencil mark until only the most perfect shape remained. It makes me feel even more out of it than my stupid new powers do.

Bree must have heard them, too, even without super-hearing, because she shrinks in her seat even more. She's taller than me by an inch or two, but right now she looks like she could disappear into thin air if she tried hard enough. I nudge her to get her attention back on me.

"Where are your mittens?" I hold up my hands and wiggle my fingers the best I can. I smirk and raise my voice just enough that it carries over to the girls. "Didn't you get the memo? Us Davis kids have to wear them to keep from spreading our poor-people germs everywhere."

The girls stop smirking at us, and their faces go all tomato red before they turn back to face the whiteboard. I take extra-special pride in shutting up Marley. I know for a fact that last summer at camp she had to wear special gloves over this cream every night for people with sweaty hands. Of course, I'd never say anything about it in public because what happens in the Shawnee Cabin stays in the Shawnee Cabin.

The bell rings, and I turn around in my seat, ready to at least pretend like I can focus with everything going on around me. But out of the corner of my eye, I catch the first Breonna Boyd smile ever on record—small, but there. It's a feat of super-natural proportions, which means I may have actually developed *two* superpowers in the past twenty-four hours. And this one, I really, really like.

8

You're never too old to play in dirt

according to my Social Studies teacher, Ms. Winston. But really, I think she just needed an excuse to check on the radishes she planted in the school garden and decided to make a whole lesson about it so she could do two things at once. She's really good at multitasking.

Our whole class is trying to plant beets as a part of Ms. Winston's lesson on the Great Famine in Ireland a long time ago. We're on our knees in the dirt, using tiny shovels to create holes in the ground for our seed pods. I'm thankful for the big gardening gloves all of us have to wear, because I'm pretty sure without them I'd get myself into trouble in a heartbeat.

The school's track is only a few feet away from the garden, so the noise from the gym class outside keeps floating over to us. They're doing circuits, which means there are a bunch of different activities that they do for a few minutes before the gym teacher, Mr. Bush, blows his whistle and they move on to the next thing. He's got big, muscular arms, a very serious face, and actually *loves* physical fitness. He's nice, but I'm convinced he must be an extraterrestrial because no one should love gym as much as he does. Well, except, Abby, I guess.

I can see Abby in her gym uniform doing back handsprings instead of jumping rope with everyone else in her circuit group. A little circle has formed around her as she does five flips in a row without even breaking a sweat. When everyone applauds her, she holds her arms out to the sides and bows. She looks around at her small audience and smiles wide. She even spots me over the heads of her classmates and jumps up and down while waving both hands in the air.

I can't help but giggle quietly. I wave one gloved hand back while Ms. Winston isn't paying attention.

"You better not be covered in mud at lunch," Abby says. She's pretending to sneeze into her elbow, but since she knows I can hear her from far away, her sneeze looks more like one of those laughs where you fart at the same time. "If a clump of dirt falls off your shirt and into my green beans, I'm suing."

This time, I laugh so loud, everyone in the garden looks over at me, including Ms. Winston.

"Sorry," I say, pretending to cough. "I'm, um, allergic to sunlight."

Ms. Winston doesn't look completely convinced, but she goes back to her lesson anyway. She corrects one of my classmates who isn't putting their seed into the ground deep enough, and I dig my gloved fingers into the soil and let myself imagine that I can touch the seeds and the leaves of the carrots in front of me with my bare hands without starting a riot or something. I try not to feel sad that it's only pretend.

"Imagine depending on food you planted with your own hands to eat," Ms. Winston says as she waves her hand over all the green leaves that have already started to pop up all over the garden.

"You can't go to the McDonald's to pick up your chicken nuggets. Everything you eat comes straight from the earth. And then"—she lowers her voice and kneels down so she's on our level—"what if the earth that you'd depended on for generations just stopped producing your food?"

Everyone in my class stops digging for a second to listen closely. We all scoot in even closer to hear Ms. Winston, whose skirt is getting stained from the ground. She doesn't even care that she's gonna be grungy for the rest of the day as long as it means she gets to spend some time in the garden, making stuff grow and bloom. She's not like any teacher I've ever seen before. They're usually so put-together, with their sweaters and their rules about not getting up and walking around and stuff.

But Ms. Winston wears flowy, patchwork dresses that look like they're from what Poppy used to call the "hippie dippy times" and always lets us play games and ask questions and do activities to help us learn.

"Almost half of the entire Irish population needed potatoes to survive, and for years, their crops were ruined," she adds. "A million people lost their lives in the famine over those years. Mothers, fathers, aunts, uncles, sisters, brothers gone because they couldn't access their main source of nutrition."

A girl named Layla with braces and brown eyes raises her hand. Her knees are extra muddy from spilling the water from the watering can over her lap earlier.

"How come they didn't just plant something else?" she asks.

Ms. Winston runs her long fingers through the damp soil and frowns. Ms. Winston is everyone's favorite teacher because she makes everything sound super important. Even if she's talking about something that happened like a billion years ago, it feels like it could have happened to one of our neighbors just a few days ago. No one even cares about being all grimy right now. Although that might be because most of my classmates are just excited to be outside in the sunshine in the middle of the day since we don't get recess anymore.

Ms. Winston looks around with her hands on her hips. She's really serious about the garden. On the first day of school, she told us that the plants she harvests outside go home with students whose families don't always have fresh veggies at their houses. I thought that was pretty cool since sometimes when the prices are too high at the grocery store, Mom puts our vegetables back on their piles and grabs the kind in cans instead. It might be nice to be able to surprise her with a bag full of tomatoes or peas or cabbage one day. Maybe we could cook them for dinner together, too.

"Well, there were lots of reasons. Lack of money, access to land, an unfriendly planting environment," Ms. Winston says, standing up and brushing off her flowy skirt. "It's important to remember that our relationship to the world around us is always give and take. It needs us and we need it. Always have. Always will." She smiles at us and then waves her hands toward the doors. "All right, that's enough for the day. You all go get washed up before the bell rings!"

My classmates throw their gloves back into the supply bag and take off to head to the bathroom sinks, but I don't get up right away. Ms. Winston walks through the row where her radishes are supposed to be popping up out of the ground right now. She looks sad as she crouches down to examine the yellowish leaves that are all curled in on themselves.

"Ms. Winston?"

She looks up and smiles at me, even though it's not a super-convincing one. It's kind of half-baked, and not in the good way that soft, melty cookies sometimes are.

"Ellie, how can I help you?"

"Are the radishes gonna get any better?" I point down at

the plant. I don't know much about gardening, but I know it's not supposed to look like that. The leaves that pop out of the ground are at least supposed to look like, well, *leaves*. Right now they mostly look like really cheap tissue paper. "Or is this kind of like what happened in the famine?"

Ms. Winston stands and places a soft hand on my shoulder. There's a little dirt under her fingernails, and the ring on her finger is all dingy from not wearing gloves during class. The scent of the soil fills my nose, and even though it could be overwhelming, I kind of like it. It reminds me that our hands can plant things that can nurture people, that we can create gardens that keep each other strong and healthy.

"Not like the famine, no. But I'm not sure these little guys are going to make it this year." Her voice sounds sad, but she tries to reassure me anyway. "It's okay, though. Bad bunches happen. I just wish we were going to have more food for take-home. Maybe next year, huh?"

Next year is a long time to wait, I think. Too long. I'm sure there are lots of people who are waiting on the food from the garden, people who need the vegetables even more than me and my mom do. Knowing that they might not get them just because of some bug in the soil or unpredictable weather or something makes my chest get a little tight.

"Is it okay if I stay out here for a minute longer?" I ask. "To make sure my seed is planted correctly?"

"Of course, kiddo. Don't stay too long, though, okay?"

Ms. Winston squeezes my shoulder. She smirks. "I gotta get you to your next class on time; otherwise that beefy gym teacher will have my head!"

I nod, but when she turns to go back inside, I don't go back to the little circle where my seed pod is planted. Instead, I move to where the neat row of shriveled-up radish leaves pokes out of the ground. I take a good look at each of them, and that same tight-chest feeling creeps up again.

"We need the earth, and the earth needs us," I whisper at the ground. "But maybe the earth needs a little more help than Ms. Winston's stinky compost fertilizer."

I take one of my gloves off and look around, back and forth down the row of radishes, and over the row of tall tomato plants in front of me. I know the bell is about to ring, so if I'm gonna do this, I've gotta be quick. I shake out my hands.

The only things I've ever resurrected were both by accident, so I have no idea what I need to do to make it happen.

"Okay, Ellie. It's now or never." I lean close to the sprout nearest me and whisper to it. "You better come back to life or so help me I'll, you know, make sure all your friends get blended into smoothies. Like, the really nasty kind. With kale."

I rub my hands together to warm them up. I don't know if I have to, but I feel like it can't hurt. I channel all my energy into my hands. I look up again, just to be safe, but this time, someone *is* looking over at me. Usually, Abby's eyes aimed in my direction make my stomach feel all fluttery, but this time, her face is frowning. The rest of her class is walking back into the gym locker room while Mr. Bush yells at them to pick up their pace, but not her.

"Ellie, I can see your brain working overtime, and I don't approve!" Abby whisper-shouts from the fence. I can only hear her because of my supersonic ears, but I don't even have time to think about how cool that is, since she looks so mad. The mind meld we've had since kindergarten gives me away, and she points at my bare hand. "I don't think that's a good idea. What if something goes wrong? What if—"

Mr. Bush blows his whistle again. "Ortega! Let's go!"

Abby rolls her eyes and stalks away while muttering, "If an army of zombie vegetables marches into the cafeteria at lunch, you're on your own."

When she disappears into the school, I take a deep breath and let it out.

"Abby's just overreacting . . ." I close my eyes. "Hopefully."

I've done this by accident before, but never on purpose or because I wanted to. I don't know what might happen, or if it'll even work when I need it to, but I have to believe it will. I place my hands on top of the damp soil and dig them into the ground. When I reach the round thing in the dirt that I think must be the dead radish, I wrap my hand around it for one second, two seconds, three seconds, and *pull!*

Right before my eyes, the dried-out sprout turns full and

reddish, like it's supposed to, and the leaves go green and perk up. I gasp and hug it to my chest.

The bell rings, but I can barely think about going to class. This is major! My whole body feels like I just stepped out into the sun after lying in the shade for too long. I can't believe I just did that. But I don't have much time. Instead of yanking the next sprout out of the ground, I tap the dry leaves and it goes from being slumped over to standing tall. My smile grows so fast and so wide I feel like my face might crack in half.

I know me and Abby talked about maybe finding a way to get rid of these powers, but as I watch each plant turn green beneath my fingertips, I realize I don't want to get rid of them. They may be scary, but they're mine. I'll just have to learn how to handle them, and when I do, who knows how much cool stuff I'll be able to do. The possibilities suddenly feel limitless.

I stand up, and just like a boxer about to enter the ring, I hold out my hand to high-five the tops of every radish sprout in the row, and they all turn green behind me. I feel like I'm floating on air. I feel powerful and strong and I don't even stop running until I reach the doors of the school.

9

I don't want to bring a rotisserie chicken back to life

but according to Abby, if I don't want to find a way to get rid of my powers, I have no choice.

"This is such a bad idea. Like, a worse idea than the time you said—"

"We don't need to talk about that!" she shouts over me to shut me up. She hates it when I bring up the hair-spray-rocket-launcher incident of third grade. That ended in lots of tears, but more important, with Abby's first and only bowl cut. It was brutal. "You did that thing in school yesterday, so obviously we have to figure this out. Who knows what could have happened with those plants!"

Abby didn't think me bringing the radishes back to life in the garden yesterday was a good idea, but she doesn't get it. She didn't feel the soft hum of power that vibrated through my fingers, the zap of energy that rushed through me when I put my hands on a dead thing and brought it back to life. And not by accident, either. On *purpose*. And she definitely doesn't know how amazing it was when Ms. Winston pulled me aside after class earlier today and held up a bag of radishes with a big, toothy smile on her face.

"I know you were worried about these yesterday," she said, shaking her head. "But I went out this morning to check on them, and they were perfect. I've never seen anything like it! Now we'll have more than enough for the harvest."

When she handed the bag to me, I couldn't help but smile a big, toothy grin right back.

"It's the strangest thing, though," she added. "Overnight, all of the tomatoes went bad. Just fell right off their vines." She shrugged. "Guess every harvest has a couple stinkers, huh?"

I didn't even know what to say back to her. I was so excited about what I was able to do that I could barely focus on anything else. It didn't even matter that I didn't know people ate radishes until yesterday! I just dropped the bag in my backpack and tried not to look like I had a lightbulb brightening me up from the inside out. I decided right away to google some radish recipes for my mom before she got home.

But Abby's reminders about how risky it was to revive the

plants, especially at school, helped me get my head back in the superhero game. There's a lot riding on me not doing anything to expose my powers, and magically healing a couple dozen dried-up radishes probably wasn't the best way to stay under the radar. Abby's right, I do need to figure out what all I can do. That way, I can't mess up. So even if I can't bring any money home to help pay bills and stuff, I can help my mom in another way. And like Ms. Winston said, a way that keeps us nourished.

Earlier, we tried to revive Monty's dirt bike. He bought it for, like, three dollars at a junkyard two months ago and has been working on the engine ever since. When it didn't magically start running, we decided that my abilities must only extend to living organisms. Plants, animals, and humans. It made me feel better to know that I wouldn't accidentally touch a broken-down chain saw one day and, well, you know... accidentally lose a finger or something.

The next phase of Abby's experiment doesn't feel like our best plan, though. I look down at the half-bones, half-meat day-old chicken carcass on the ground in front of us. We're sitting in the dirt of Mrs. Ortega's abandoned gardening project, hidden behind a big, overgrown bush that I think is supposed to bloom roses, but really just looks like a giant weed. It's the most private place we have. After the radish experiment, Abby figured it was time to go big or go home.

Hence the Great Plainsboro Chicken Resurrection. I'd

probably feel a little bit like Jesus if I weren't currently so nervous that my pit stains have pit stains.

"Okay." Abby takes a deep breath and frowns. Her voice sounds extra dramatic as she stares at the chicken. "The moment of truth has arrived."

She's right. Mrs. Ortega is inside with the twins and the baby, Monty is upstairs on the phone with his girlfriend, Mr. Ortega is at the grocery store, and my mom will be home in an hour. This is it.

I close my eyes, take off one mitten, and slowly move my hand closer to the chicken. My face screws up like I'm smelling something seriously rank, and pictures of a zombie chicken with no eyes, no face, and no feathers, squawking around the garage and feasting on our brains like lunch meat, flash through my mind. I'm gonna be singlehandedly responsible for the real-life version of that horrible Willa Moon movie, *The Undead Ate My Mother.* I shiver at the thought.

"Oh, come on!" Abby says, and my eyes snap open to stare her down.

"If you had the power to raise the dead before you were even old enough to get your learner's permit, I bet you'd be a little freaked out about your first intentional fowl resurrection, too!" I whisper-shout in her direction.

"I haven't even seen you do it yet." Abby shrugs and crosses her arms. "Maybe you don't even *have* any powers."

Ugh. Abby always does this. Says she doesn't believe I can

do something just so I have no choice but to prove her wrong. It's how she got me to jump out of the tree in her backyard when we were seven, and the way she got me to ride on the handlebars of her powder-blue Huffy when we were ten. I broke my wrist jumping out of the tree and fell off her bike and skinned my knee so bad I still have the scar to prove it.

It's probably not a good idea to let that make me touch the chicken. But I do.

We both scream when I tap it so hard little bits of meat fly everywhere. Abby dives into the bush to get away, and I curl up in a ball like an armadillo. It isn't until Mrs. Ortega pops her head out the back door to see what all the noise is about that we realize the chicken isn't moving.

"Abigail! What is all that noise?" she calls over the yard.

Abby slides out from under the bush quickly. There's a big green grass stain on her jeans.

"Look at your pants!" Mrs. Ortega puts her hand on her forehead like Abby does when she freaks out. "And is that my chicken? Nope. I don't want to know. That's enough. Both of you better clean this mess up or so help me you'll wish you could trade places with that chicken."

I have no idea what that means, but I take it seriously enough to not want to push our luck.

"We better go in," I say, shrugging. I can stick to dying veggies from here on out. No problem. "I think we get the general idea, right?"

"What if..." Abby jerks her head toward the tree behind her and I groan. She starts explaining before I have a chance to tell her that she's officially flown the cuckoo's nest. "No, listen! I think this is the ultimate test. If you can bring Bunny back to life, then we know that your powers can revive..."

"Skeletons?"

Abby nods. "Exactly!"

I shake my head.

This is so bad. Bunny was Abby's pet guinea pig from kindergarten to first grade. His name was a pretty unfortunate inaccuracy, but he was really sweet. Too sweet, I guess. Because one day, Monty's pet python, Spike, escaped his cage, slithered his way into Abby's room, and things weren't too pretty. The Ortegas put a memorial under the tree in their backyard for Spike when he passed away, but seeing as Bunny was still stuck in his digestive tract at the time, it was a two-for-one burial.

I crawl over to the patch of dirt where a small rock with Spike's and Bunny's names written on it in faded paint sits. I kneel and think about whether any comic book I've ever read has dealt with the consequences of disturbing a double pet grave. I can't come up with any examples, but something tells me it's an even worse plan than the chicken revival.

I don't think of myself as a brave person. I mean, I don't think I'm some big scaredy-cat, I just mean that doing new stuff has never been all that interesting to me. I even hate when we have to go outside for gym class. It's too big of a change. I *like* the comfort of being surrounded by four walls. I *like* the too-cold chill of school air-conditioning forcing you to bring a jacket to school, even in the summer. I *like* having a chair for my butt and a desk for my books and the most unpredictable thing each day being what the lunch ladies will believe qualifies as food. All that is thrown out the window when you go outdoors.

But Abby has always made me want to be braver. Even when I didn't think I could, she's always believed it was possible. Even little stuff.

Like when we were in first grade, and she learned I didn't know how to ride my bike without training wheels yet. I didn't think I could do it, and my parents didn't really want to try and teach me because they were worried I would get hurt. But, at the beginning of summer, Abby forced Monty to take the training wheels off my bike so she could teach me how. For a long time, just like my parents feared, I was really bad at it.

"Maybe you two babies should just give up!" Monty yelled from the porch.

"Go bother someone else, toe-jam breath!" she yelled back while she helped me up. Then she put her hands on her hips and said, "Ignore him. Now try again."

My mom and dad didn't understand why I kept going outside for lessons every day even though I was all scraped up. They still thought all I could do was cry when things weren't going my way, just like I used to when they dropped me off at school in kindergarten. They didn't try to get me into Little League (the balls flew too fast) or Girl Scouts (anything could happen in the woods) or 4-H (too much craft glitter and too many unruly barnyard animals). It was like they wrapped me up in Bubble Wrap and kept me far away from anything that could hurt me.

But Abby had fallen off her bike before. She knew that once you got past the scraped knees, there was something way cooler on the other side. And she wanted me to know it, too.

"It's okay to be afraid, Ellie-Welly," she said, slapping my third Band-Aid of the day on my arm. She said she wanted to be in the Olympics one day, but I thought she would make a good nurse. "But my gymnastics coach says if you don't try anyway, you'll never be the best. And you're already the best friend ever, so I'm sure you can be the best at this, too!"

I rode my bike without falling off for the first time that day and rode everywhere in our neighborhood for the rest of the summer. It was the greatest feeling ever. Riding the bike was fun, but the best part was knowing that even when no one else thought I could do it, Abby believed in me. She may have always been the first between us to try new things, or develop new hobbies, but I was always right there behind her, trying to catch up. And she always believed that I could.

I know Abby believes in my powers, too. She knows they're real and that them getting out is a big problem. It's exactly why she thinks I should hide them, and why we're doing all this to figure out how to control them, right? That's me and Abby's thing. We look out for each other. I have to believe that this is just her way of doing that, even if I don't think it's our smartest plan.

I look over at her, and she nods once.

"I think this is our only choice," she says.

She keeps using the word *our* like she's the one about to become a preteen gravedigger, but I'm the person who has to do all the dirty work around here. Literally. She runs to the garage and returns with the tiny shovel her mom used to use to plant her garden before she gave up on growing flowers completely. Abby places a hand on my shoulder and holds the shovel out to me. Her lips are pressed together seriously.

"Don't you want to know what's going on in those hands of yours?" she asks.

She kneels down beside me, and she's so close I could count each of her eyelashes if I wanted to. When she looks at me like this, like I'm the only person in the world, I never know whether I want to run and hide or stay frozen in place forever so she'll never look away. It makes my head feel kind of fuzzy in the way it gets after spinning in circles too many times.

I know I'm gonna say yes before the word comes out of my mouth just because of Abby nodding her encouragement. I don't think I could say no even if I knew doing what she's asking me to do would unleash Panera's box or whatever.

When I nod, Abby smiles, and it feels like the first ray of summer sun hitting your skin after a rainy spring. It's enough to make me forget about how ridiculous it is to dig up her big brother's pet snake and his last supper.

"This is illegal, I think," I say, digging in and tossing dirt to the side. "I'm sure it is, actually. There are definitely laws against grave robbing."

"It's not robbery if it's a grave in your own backyard. Everybody knows that." She shrugs like that's just common knowledge, and I make a mental note to ask my mom about it later. "Oh my gosh, look!"

She reaches into the shallow hole and pulls out the dirty, disintegrating shoebox coffin.

"Bunny!" She clutches the box to her chest like Willa Moon holding a box of her boyfriend's old love letters after he dumps her in her movie *Letters from Ipanema*. "I'm so sorry I couldn't protect you!"

"Aren't you the one who forgot to close his cage, which is how Spike got in there in the first place?" I ask.

Abby ignores me and shoves the box into my hands. "Here! I can't bear to look at it."

I set the box down on the ground and take a deep breath.

"I think we should pray," I say.

Abby's face screws up in confusion. "Do you know any prayers?"

"Not really." Besides the one I used to memorialize Burt the Betta Fish, I'm coming up short. "But shouldn't we ask a higher power for permission or something?"

"Ellie." Abby lays a hand on my arm. Her voice is soft like she's a preschool teacher telling her students not to eat glue or something. "*Teen Scene* says that life isn't about asking permission."

Abby's right. Well, she's not right about the *Teen Scene* thing, because there's tons of stuff in life you should definitely ask permission for before doing, but she is right about just getting this over with. I grab the edge of the dirt-covered top, peel it up slowly, and—

"Oh my god!"

The top explodes off like a shaken-up can of soda, and the two of us fall back on our butts. Instead of a reanimated skeleton, a furious gopher that's chewed its way into the box jumps out and dashes over Abby's chest and leaps into her ponytail. We're both shrieking so loud I'm sure if my fumbling fingers don't manage to bring back Bunny, our voices are enough to wake the dead.

"Ellie! Get it off me!"

Abby rolls around in the grass, kicking and screaming. I don't know what to do, so I grab the thing closest to me, the shoebox coffin, and throw it at the gopher. He dodges out of the way and scurries up the tree, but Bunny's bones scatter and land all over Abby's brand-new tank top. If she wasn't screaming before, the noise that comes out of her mouth in that moment sounds so much like an ambulance siren that I'm sure there's an emergency nearby.

I reach over to dust the bones off of her, but Abby immediately sprints into the house, shrieking in horror the whole way. I run after her as she takes the stairs two at a time and locks herself in the bathroom. Since I'm not really sure what you're supposed to do when your best friend has been doused in guinea pig bones, I just leave a change of clothes for her outside the door and wait for her in her room.

When she comes back out twenty minutes later, her skin looks pink from how hard she's scrubbed it, and her hair is freshly blow-dried. It looks like she ran herself through the washing machine in a double spin cycle when she plops down next to me on her bed. We both fall back on the mattress and stare at the ceiling. Okay, so it wasn't our best plan, but at least we know more now than we did before.

"That was horrible," Abby says with a giggle after a second. I guess the shower was enough time to recover from the shock. "I'll never be able to look at a chicken, or bones, the same way again."

I can't help but laugh, too. We may not know everything, but at least we got that out of the way. I can't bring back food that's been cooked. And since I touched the bones when trying to dust them off of her and they didn't immediately come back to life, it doesn't look like I can revive something that doesn't still have all the necessary parts of a body like a heart and a brain and stuff.

"I don't think you should use your powers when I'm not around, just in case," she says, patting my arm. "Who knows what might happen if I can't be there to help you."

I press my lips together and try to find words to respond. I mean, I can't only use my powers when Abby's around, right? Captain America doesn't limit his super-strength when Bucky Barnes isn't right by his side. Wolverine doesn't put his super-healing abilities on the back burner when Kitty Pryde isn't there.

I sigh. There are still too many questions, and every answer only makes me wonder more.

I look over at Abby, who's holding her phone above her face. The glow from the screen makes her cheeks look like one of those influencers sitting in front of a ring light. She's smiling at something while she scrolls, but it's a smile that's usually saved for goofy jokes between the two of us, never strangers. The sight of it makes it feel hard to breathe.

"What's so funny?"

The first thing Abby does when she reads something funny online is shove her phone in my face so I can laugh, too, but this time she's so focused on whatever it is she doesn't even hear me ask.

"Huh?"

I feel silly for the way my face gets hot when I have to repeat myself, even though it shouldn't be embarrassing to have to say something again when someone doesn't hear you. But I guess that's normal with Abby nowadays. I'm always trying to squash one weird feeling or another.

"I *said* something must be pretty funny, 'cause you're laughing without even making noise, which you only do when you watch those big animal–little animal best-friend videos."

"Oh yeah." Her thumbs fly across the screen as she types. "Marley just texted me. At callouts yesterday, this girl— Well, never mind, you kind of had to be there, but it was hilarious. She just sent me this meme that reminded her of it."

I sit up and shake my head a little, like that will help me get rid of the too-warm feeling in my cheeks. It's okay that Abby and Marley have inside jokes or whatever. Me and Abby have a lot of inside jokes that we've laughed about millions of times. But knowing that doesn't change the fact that I wish I could revive a crusty chicken carcass and throw it straight through Marley's bedroom window. I know it's not the best use of my supernatural abilities, but it would be fun to watch her get so freaked out she peed her pants a little.

I grab my backpack from the floor and hike it up my shoulders. I forgot about the radishes while we were doing our experiments, but I probably need to put them in the fridge or something.

Mental note to self: Google how to store radishes after you google how to eat radishes after you google "Are radishes even a real vegetable?"

"I gotta go," I say.

Abby finally looks up from her phone and frowns. "What? Why? I thought we were gonna paint our nails!"

Really, Abby was probably gonna paint my nails and then complain about painting her own nails because I have "no eye for the intricacies of nail design." It's usually fun. But I don't want to do it tonight anymore. It's weird, I always want to spend time with Abby. But there's a lot of stuff I have to figure out on my own right now, I think. She can help me sort out how my powers work, but I'm the one who has to live with them. I haven't really decided what that means yet, but I get the feeling Abby's not the person to ask.

"Can't. Gotta feed Burt the Betta Fish 2.0." I shrug. "Maybe tomorrow?"

Abby hops up and gives me a firm hug before I leave, making me swear not to bring anything back to life while she's not around to supervise.

"I promise," I say, rolling my eyes. "We're in this together forever, right?"

She smiles and puts her hands on both of my shoulders before squeezing tight.

"Forever and two days."

10

Every boy in our grade looks like a gigantic toe

and yet all the girls in Language Arts can't stop talking about them. Well, one in particular—Sammy Spencer.

Sammy has curly blond hair and icy-blue eyes and rosy cheeks and the kind of face that looks more like a doll's than a real boy's. Instead of paying attention while Mrs. Harlow taught her lesson in class today, everyone passed notes that I'm as sure as any girl with super-senses could be were about him. And I didn't want to focus on it, or his doll face, but they whispered his name so loudly, it was all I could focus on.

Instead of learning about the difference between similes

and metaphors, all I heard the entire period was "Oh my god, Sammy looks like such an angel!" and "I heard he only kisses girls with green eyes!" and "I bet if we get married, we would be the next Willa Moon and Cal Key!" It made me so frustrated that by the time I got to Abby's locker after class, I thought I might spontaneously combust.

And then Abby says his name, and I think I might actually see the pearly gates.

"He said *Hey*. Can you believe it?" She reaches into the backpack hanging in her locker and grabs her new Willa Moon "Moonshine" lip gloss. Her cheeks are pink, and her voice is all high and squeaky. "Sammy Spencer said *Hey*, to me, outside the library!"

A week ago, we didn't even *know* Sammy. He was just another fancy-pants kid from the other side of town in a fancy-pants house with a super-green yard and one of those driveways that loops around for no reason. So what if he actually did the summer reading and has a Captain America pin on his backpack and calls the teacher *ma'am* like his parents actually taught him some manners? He just wants to get everyone to think he's innocent. But I know a villain when I see one.

When I don't answer right away, Abby just keeps going, almost like she's having a conversation with herself.

"Don't forget, I have cheerleading tryouts after school today, so I probably won't see you again until tomorrow."

She puckers her lips in the magnetic mirror she put inside

her locker yesterday. The gloss looks a little too sticky to me, but she seems to like it. She started practicing different makeup looks over the summer with a lot of help from YouTube videos. Abby can't draw at all—her self-portrait in third-grade art class was so horrendously blobby and blocky at the same time that our art teacher thought maybe she needed glasses if that's what she thought she looked like. But she treats her face the way I treat my comic books—like a work of art.

Watching her spend the summer learning to do wild eye-shadow combinations and how to make her nose look like it was a whole different shape with concealer was like watching an artist learn to paint. Sometimes the portrait came out flawless, and sometimes it still needed some work. But always, because it's Abby, the canvas was perfect.

She practices a smile in her reflection and then turns it on me. "Do I look cheerleader-y enough?"

I lean against the cold metal and shove my hands in my pockets, since it's kind of hard to keep them from looking all jittery.

Ever since this *thing* happened to me, my hands and feet are always buzzy, like I could run a mile and not get tired. My ears feel like they're filled with cotton, muddy with all the sounds of the people around me. Between classes is the worst. Lockers slamming are cannons, booming every five seconds, and all the feet against the shiny floors are an unstoppable stampede. I wish I still had my earmuffs, but Abby refuses to give them back. So, while she talks, I try to shut out everything except the sound of her voice.

If I think hard enough, it almost doesn't feel that different from usual.

"What is a cheerleader supposed to look like?"

"You know, like—" She looks up at the ceiling to think until she figures out what she wants me to see. She shuts her locker with a loud *click* and doesn't seem to notice when I jump a little.

"Got it! Willa Moon in *Pep Squad by Day, Pop Star by Night*! I bet Sammy would love that movie. Oh my gosh, he's your lab partner, right? Do you think you could ask him about me?"

I nod, but I'm not really listening anymore. My ears are ringing, and I just want to get out of the hallway.

"Ew, oh my gosh do you see that?" Abby shrieks.

She points at the entrance to the girls' bathroom by the nurse's office. It's the worst bathroom in the school because the pipes always leak and creepy-crawlies hang out in the corners. I follow Abby's finger to where a dead roach lies belly-up right in a puddle of leaky sink water near the entrance. Normally, I'd be grossed out right alongside her, but I can't even think about the nastiness of a dead bug. Not when Sammy Spencer is skyrocketing to the top of my list of Least Favorite People on the Face of This Wretched Earth.

Stupid Sammy Spencer with his stupid angelic face and his stupid gemstone eyes and his stupid *Hey*. Who even says that? I'm way cooler than Sammy Spencer. I have *powers*! And sure, no one knows I have them, and I'm not entirely sure how they work, but still!

Then, like an angel dropped a girl-sized stink bomb right there in front of us, Bethany Thomas rounds the corner, and a lightbulb goes off in my head. Bethany is always giving Abby a hard time at gymnastics and beat her out for a spot at Junior Nationals last year. She's Abby's mortal enemy, which means she's my mortal enemy, too, as is dictated by best friend law.

If ever there was a time to use my powers to show Abby how cool they are, and how much cooler I am than Sammy, this is it.

Bethany rounds the corner to the girls' bathroom, and I tap Abby on the shoulder.

"Hey, follow me," I whisper.

We're supposed to be headed to lunch, but I quietly trail after Bethany as she enters the bathroom. We peek around the doorframe and spot Bethany straightening her sweater in the mirror. She seems way less intimidating now than she does marching out of the Rising Phoenix gym in her leotard and glitter every Saturday when I wait for Abby to get done with practice. I usually don't pay any attention to Bethany aside from when Abby wants to complain about her landing a stunt before she does, or when she says a mean comment about Abby's hair or body or something. But.

"What are we doing?" Abby whispers.

I shush her just as Bethany disappears into a stall. I raise my eyebrows as I point at the dead roach on the ground and then at the stall, hoping she gets the right idea. I know it clicks when her eyes get wide and her smile shows off that one crooked tooth of hers. The way she's smiling at me, I know she's not thinking of Sammy Spencer, or even her cool new friend, Marley. It's just the two of us.

That's all I need to gather enough gumption to get over how incredibly disgusting touching a dead bug is. I kneel down and pinch my nose with one hand, just in case my super-smell makes it too rank to get close to.

"This is gonna be too good." Abby giggles behind me.

And just like that, I wrap my hand around the roach, and immediately feel a buzz of energy pulse through me as his little legs start squirming in my hand. I can't stand the feel of him wiggling around in my palm for another second, so I rush into the bathroom, throw the bug over the stall door Bethany walked into, and run.

"WHAT THE HECK IS THAT!"

Bethany screams bloody murder, and Abby doubles over in laughter. I grab her wrist to pull her out of the bathroom so we don't get caught, but I completely forget about the tiny pond that's forming by the door thanks to the leaky sink. My foot slips and both of my legs go flying into the air, taking Abby down with me. Then, as if things couldn't get any worse, Bethany throws open her stall door and sprints out. But, thanks to the intrusion of a roach on her head, she doesn't see us flailing around on the ground.

Her sandal catches on Abby's ponytail, and just like that, she lands face-first in the massive heap that is me and Abby.

"My eye!" Abby yells when Bethany elbows her in the face as she tries to stand.

"My leg!" Bethany whines as Abby knocks her knee into Bethany's shin.

Mrs. Morales from science chooses that exact moment to appear above us, hands on her hips and DETENTION written all over her face.

I flop back on the ground and groan.

"My dignity."

I get a cupcake in my face

almost as soon as I walk through the door of Patty's Cakes.
Mr. Walker sets it on the little checkered-top table in the corner where I always sit. Where my poppy used to sit, too, back
when he was alive. The vanilla cupcake with white-and-yellow
swirled icing probably isn't the best snack to eat when I know
dinner is in a little while, but I take a huge bite out of it anyway.

"Thanks, Mr. Walker," I say when I'm done chewing. I try
to smile, but it must look pretty pitiful, because instead of disappearing back into the kitchen like he usually does, he sits
down across from me.

"Did my mom make this?"

He nods once and pokes one gloved finger in my forehead

where my eyebrows are smushed together in the middle. I laugh. I don't think I've ever even seen Mr. Walker bake; I just know that he does. It's hard to imagine him doing anything that requires him to take his gloves off.

Poppy told me once that Mr. Walker talked a lot back before the war in Vietnam, but when they came back, he was different. Still gentle, still kind, but he didn't say much anymore. Not that it matters, I guess, because Mr. Walker has the biggest, bushiest gray eyebrows ever, and they say more than words could anyway.

Right now, they bob up once, and I know that means I should tell him what's going on if I feel like it.

"It's stupid." I shake my head. I lick some of the icing off my thumb and shrug.

And it *is* stupid. I feel like a baby for even being annoyed about it. But. When the cheerleading roster got posted after school yesterday, I was happy for Abby. I swear I was. I want her to do everything she wants to do. I mean, she can already out-flip and out-pep any of the other girls on the team! It's good. It's just . . . I miss her.

I hate it because I just saw her today at school, so I shouldn't feel that way, but I don't know. It's all the small stuff. Like how Marley Keilor was at her locker after school, and they were laughing at another joke I didn't understand. And when I asked about it, Marley looked at me like I was a stinkbug on her boot and said, "It's an insider. From tryouts? You wouldn't get it."

Abby has always been the one person who thought it was cool that I read comic books instead of watching Netflix or that I would rather hang out with my poppy than go to our classmates' birthday parties. She had her thing and I had mine. We met in the middle, and the middle was us. Together. Laughing about Monty freaking out over his first date, or trying to build a balance beam in the Ortegas' backyard with branches that fell during a storm, or making fun of the boys whose voices started to randomly squeak in the middle of a sentence at the end of sixth grade.

I thought we didn't need other people. But I guess I was wrong. *I* didn't need other people. For Abby, just me isn't enough.

And it doesn't help that she had to miss the first day of practice today for our detention. Even though it wasn't completely my fault, Abby shot me daggers the entire time we were there. So it's safe to say that the lunchtime incident backfired harder than Monty's crappy motorcycle does.

"Did you ever think that you and Poppy were too different to be friends?" I ask Mr. Walker now.

He and my poppy were besties back in the day. They grew up together, went into the army together, and eventually moved back to Plainsboro to do what every adult does: get a boring job and start a boring family. Mr. Walker opened the bakery, and Poppy married Gramma Candy and they had my mom.

Poppy used to say Mr. Walker wouldn't know his booty from his cue-ball head if he weren't around to tell him what was what. But when Poppy got old and retired from his job at the car factory, he would sit at one of the tables in front of the bakery and complain all day. I would sit in a booster seat across from him or, when I was old enough, stand behind the counter counting change for Mr. Walker while Poppy hooted and hollered about how the cold weather made his bones ache, or how the new Marvel story lines were too predictable, or how Mr. Walker's red velvet cake couldn't possibly taste as good as Gramma Candy's.

But he always winked at me while he did it, like nothing else was as fun as being loud and cranky while Mr. Walker just smiled and ignored him. Mr. Walker was the quiet one, Poppy was the wild one. They balanced each other out.

I never knew my grandparents on my dad's side, but that was okay. I still sort of ended up with two grandpas. And since Mr. Walker never had any kids of his own, I try to visit whenever I can now that Poppy's gone, even if it's just to sit in the front of the bakery and do my homework. That way he knows he's still part of our family.

"Hm," he huffs. His voice sounds like a car driving over gravel when he answers. "Being different ain't bad. Makes you grow."

Mr. Walker is an incredible listener. He's probably the best person I could talk to about everything that's going on right now. He wouldn't understand it, but he would at least not look at me like I'd grown two heads and was speaking fluent French when I told him that I'm suddenly super, like Abby did. It would feel good to tell an adult, right? Isn't that what you're supposed to do when you have a problem too big to handle on your own?

I open my mouth to explain that my "being different" is worse than just being taller than my classmates or whatever other health-class all-bodies-are-good-bodies bullet points he might be thinking up. But the second I do, Mr. Walker's eyebrows shoot up in that easy way of his, like he's nudging me to continue, and the words get stuck in my throat like an oversized gumball.

I sigh. There's no way I can tell him the truth. The last thing I want is for him to think I'm losing my mind, or worse, that I'm a liar. I shake my head and look down.

"I don't think I like it. Growing. Changing."

I pick at a scratch on the table. *Changing* is the understatement of the year.

"Well, the only way out is through," he starts, repeating Poppy's favorite line. He pushes himself back from the table and stands up. He adds, "Seems like change is just in the air these days."

He knocks his fist against the countertop twice and cocks his head to the side. He looks at me like he sometimes looks at a fancy cake he has to decorate with complicated pastel flowers and loopy script.

"Tell me about it." I sigh. "I'm only twelve, but I gotta say, I'm ready to retire. Poppy had it made. Nothing ever changed for him. He got to hang out with his best friend all day and read comic books at night. That's the life."

Mr. Walker lets out a quiet laugh. "Your poppy was a creature of habit, that's for certain."

He points to the window at the front of the shop. They were able to replace it the very next day after it shattered in the earthquake, but the logo on the glass—the one that Poppy and Mr. Walker had hand-painted together all those years ago—couldn't be saved. Now, instead of the kind of lopsided, chipping bubble script, there's perfectly crisp vinyl letters that spell out PATTY'S CAKES. It's really nice, I guess. New. But it's not the same.

I'm becoming an expert in that department. I know really well how something can be cool and terrible at the same time.

"But not all changes are scary," he says. He adjusts his gloves over his hands like he does sometimes when he thinks too hard. "Even if they seem that way at first."

He jerks his head in the direction of the door, his signal that I should flip the OPEN sign to CLOSED to mark the end of the day. When I do, he hands me a broom and I start sweeping up the front. It's kind of nice to have something to focus on that's not how I feel right now.

As I sweep, I think about my mom doing the same thing here when she was my age. She started with a broom, got promoted to the register when she was a teenager, and started baking while she went to college. It all seems so normal when

I think about it. Cleaning up, counting change, creating cake towers for weddings. The same thing every day, no surprises. When Mr. Walker flips off the light and offers to drive me home, I can't help but think there's something really great about normal.

And that, if I had one wish, a normal life would be the only thing worth asking for.

12

Since there are no flash cards for new necromancers

to study how to hone their skills, I'm kind of out on my own. But never let it be said that Ellie Engle isn't resourceful. Because if there's one thing I learned to do a long time ago, it's how to make lemonade with lemons. And sure, sometimes the lemons are rotten, and the sugar is weird and clumpy, but you can still make lemonade. I wouldn't sell it at a lemonade stand or anything because people would definitely ask for refunds, but . . .

Okay, none of that is the point.

The point is, I have work to do. When I walk into the hardware store on Main Street after school, I'm a girl on a mission. Yesterday, Mr. Walker said all change doesn't have to be bad, so I try to imagine my powers and everything that comes with them being a good thing. And when I think about them less like a punishment and more like a weird (and totally uncalled for) gift, then they're not so bad at all. My entire life I've wondered what it might be like to have superpowers, and now I kind of have no choice but to figure it out.

So I'm starting with the basics: seeds.

I don't know much about gardening, but I know seeds grow into plants that become food. Food that we don't have to buy at the grocery store, which saves my mom a little bit of the money that she has to spend on me. The other day, she was so surprised by the radishes (and the recipe I found on Google!) that she shoved the frozen dinners we were gonna eat back in the freezer and roasted the radishes in butter and garlic and sprinkled them with cheese. It only took a few minutes, and it was so delicious we both had two plates full.

I felt so good, so helpful, that it made me think maybe I could keep doing stuff like that. You don't need the power of necromancy to have a garden—although I'm taking notes on the gardens that look too good around town because they might be worth adding to my list of superhero suspects—but it will probably help. But I'm gonna need a lot of expert assistance first.

"Excuse me," I say to the lady in the gardening section. She's wearing overalls and a bandanna like gardeners always do on TV, so I figure she probably knows a lot about plants and stuff. "Could you help me find these?"

I hand her a list of my favorite vegetables, the ones that I want to grow. I've already found a good spot for them in the backyard and everything, right in the patch of grass that gets a lot of sunlight in the afternoons. We learned about photosynthesis in science a while back. Sun is crucial to feed plants, as crucial as water is to humans.

The lady turns around with narrowed eyes and takes the list from my hand. She reads it over without saying anything and then grunts.

"Young people these days don't know jack about the outdoors," she says, shaking her head. "All you kids care about is video games. You can't plant any of this this late in the year." She shoves the list back in my hand. "Try again next spring."

The overalls lady goes back to pressing price stickers on the spray paint cans on the shelf and my heart deflates. I feel like shrinking. I can't believe I really thought I could start a whole garden just by buying a few packets of seeds. I guess it was a bad idea. I shuffle toward the door and start thinking up other ways to put my powers to use. Maybe I can become a kid detective who brings people back to life just to find out who killed them! I bet that pays a lot.

Eh, it's probably too messy, I think. *And bodily fluids make me want to puke.*

"Ellie?"

My head shoots up at Ms. Winston's familiar voice behind me. She's not wearing the dress and ballet flats she had on in class today; now she's got on a pair of ripped jean shorts, colorful high-tops, and a T-shirt for something called riot grrrl. I know teachers have lives outside of school and stuff, but seeing her in jean shorts is just a step too far. It's casual Friday, but don't old people have some kind of permanent dress code?

"What are you doing here?" she asks, smiling wide. "Building something?"

I shrug, remembering my stupid plan.

"I was gonna start a garden," I say. "Kind of like the one at school. But it was a dumb idea. I don't know anything about that kind of stuff."

All I know about is comic books and superheroes and that information isn't coming in handy right now. If I can't even figure out how to get something as tiny as a seed to turn into food, then how in the world am I ever gonna figure out how to work my powers?

"What do you mean? That's a great idea." Ms. Winston claps her hands together. "I can help! Or better yet ..." She turns and calls over her shoulder. "Parker, come here!"

And like Ms. Winston summoned them out of thin air, someone walks out of the cleaning supply aisle with a bucket full of sponges and carpet cleaner. They drop the bucket on the ground when they reach us and wrap an arm around Ms. Winston's waist.

"P, this is Ellie, one of my star pupils." She winks at me. "Ellie, this is my partner, Parker."

"Nice to meet you, Ellie!" Parker holds out a hand for me to shake and smiles. "If Ness says you're a star pupil, you must really be something special. She's a tough judge."

"Well, I don't know...." I suddenly feel kind of shy. I'm a good student and all, but I'm not a *star*. I just like how it feels to know lots of information, so I pay close attention in class. Nothing special about that. "She's a really good teacher, though."

"You're so sweet!" Ms. Winston says, blushing when Parker kisses her on the cheek. "P, I was just telling Ellie you're a pro at gardening. She could use some tips on how to get started." She turns to me and adds, "P is the one who helped me start the garden at school. I'd be lost without them!"

Parker reaches for my crumpled list, and I give it to them, feeling embarrassed all over again. Now Ms. Winston and her partner are both gonna know how unprepared I really am to do something I've never done before. One of the reasons why I stick to what I know is because it's easier that way. If you don't have to learn anything new, you don't make as many mistakes. Everyone knows that. It's just simpler not to do anything new in the first place, I figure.

"Oh yeah, this is a great start!" Parker says, marching toward the gardening section. "But see, a lot of crops are seasonal, so you gotta plant 'em at just the right time. A good lesson on life, I say. A thing can be perfectly good, but if it comes at the wrong time, then it just doesn't quite work out."

Parker stops in front of a shelf full of packets of seeds and bags of these things called bulbs. There's so much, I have no idea where to even start looking, let alone what I would start growing first. But Parker seems to know everything.

"Spinach is perfect. It does really well in fall weather." Parker hands a packet of spinach seeds to me, then stands on their tiptoes to reach the shelf above their head. "Turnips are great! You'll have no trouble with those. And, oh yeah, your first lettuce harvest will change your life. I cried when my little green guys were ready to go, and . . ."

Parker gets so excited that they just keep grabbing and grabbing until my arms are piled high with seeds and supplies. When I can barely see over them and think I might just topple over in the middle of the store, Ms. Winston chimes in.

"P," she says with a laugh. "I think Ellie has more than enough to get started, don't you?"

"Oh!" Parker turns around and their cheeks get pink as they scratch the back of their neck. "I get a little carried away when talking about fall harvests. They're just so much fun!"

I follow Ms. Winston and Parker to the register, wondering

how in the world I thought my five dollars from sweeping up Patty's Cakes yesterday was gonna be enough for all this stuff. I'm doing the math in my head and getting more and more nervous the higher the total climbs as the cashier scans each item. Parker and Ms. Winston stand behind me with their bucket, chattering about how great it is I'm starting a garden and how deep I should plant each seed and when I can expect to see them start to come in, and when the cashier reaches the end of my items, they place theirs on the counter next.

I appreciate all the help, but if they think I can buy their stuff *and* mine, they are way overestimating the reach of my part-part-part-time job.

I open my mouth to tell them just as Parker hands over their credit card.

"What are you doing?" I ask.

"Just helping you get started," they say. The cashier hands my bags to me, and Parker nudges me toward the door as I try to hand over my five-dollar bill to pay them back. "Keep it for spring seeds. Consider this a kick start from one gardener to another, huh?"

"If your touch is half as magical at home as it was with those radishes at school, you'll have nothing to worry about," Ms. Winston says as she ruffles the top of my head.

The two of them wave good-bye as I place my bags in the basket on my handlebars. I scrub at my eyes with the back of my hand as I watch them go to stop myself from doing something silly like tearing up in the hardware store parking lot. But as I pedal home, I make myself a promise. The first two plants I grow, I'm giving to Ms. Winston and Parker.

*

Dirty hands make for a clean home, as Poppy used to say when we were cleaning. And my hands are currently so dirty, the home my new plants are growing into has got to be the cleanest that's ever been. The second I got back from the store, I rushed to the patch of grass that I dedicated to my garden and got to work. I never thought I would be into the feeling of mud soaking through my jeans and dirt clumping under my fingernails or sweat dripping down my neck, but I *am*.

I feel like a forest creature, or better yet, an Ewok from those old Star Wars movies. Cute but with undoubtedly subpar hygiene.

Grime and all, I feel clearer out here. The fog that feels like it's been following me ever since I got my powers starts to fade with each hole I dig and each seed I plant. There's just something so cool about knowing that I'm starting something today that will last for longer than the time it takes for me to do it. Something that requires patience and tenderness. Like waiting for a new issue of my favorite comic to come out or handling a vintage issue with care so I don't rip the pages.

After I drop the last spinach seed into the ground and cover it with dirt, I peel off my new gardening gloves and run my hands over the yellowing, dried-out grass in this part of the yard. I watch it turn green under my fingertips. A small burst of energy shoots through me as I bring it to life, and it feels the same way it felt when I did it at school the other day, only better, because this time there's no rush. No one can see into our yard, and there's no bell about to ring for class, so I can take all the time I want.

"Ellie!" Abby shouts, vaulting herself over our side of the fence instead of just walking through.

"Hey!" I call over my shoulder, and brush the dirt off my knees. "How was cheerleading?"

Abby still has her hair in a high ponytail from practice and a sour look on her face, so I have a feeling I know the answer before she says it.

"I have to be a base for the lifts," she says, crossing her arms. "Even though I have more experience with tumbling than any of the other girls! It's stupid." She frowns when she sees the patch of dirt in front of me. "What are you doing?"

I smile. "Gardening! I bought seeds and talked to Ms. Winston and her partner about what grows best in the fall and—"

"Are you using your powers?" she asks, voice low. She steps closer to me and puts her hands on her hips. "Without me here? I thought we agreed that was a bad idea!"

No, I think, you *agreed, and I didn't say anything.*

"Well, I haven't used them that much." I shrug. I stand up and brush myself off. "Besides, no one was gonna see me. I was just back here in the yard."

I kneel down to pick up a puffy dandelion and hold it up between us. Usually, I'd blow and make a wish, and the seeds would scatter into the wind, but this is much cooler.

"Watch this," I say. I cup my hand over the top for a second and let the zing of energy that comes from a revival zip through me and pull my hand back like a magician. Just like I predicted, it's sunny yellow, and good as new. "Ta-da! I figured out that I can do this with any plant as long as it hasn't lost any petals or seeds yet. I can do it with tons of stuff now, whenever I want. Isn't that cool?"

Abby presses her lips together like she wants to say something but doesn't know how. I don't know why she's acting so weird, I mean, hasn't she been talking about how I need to learn how to use my powers? Well, this is the way to do it, by practicing! I'm getting better at knowing what my hands can do, and I'm kind of enjoying being able to do it. Maybe a few days ago, I was scared of my powers, but I'm not scared anymore. Still a little weirded out, sure, but not scared. So, Abby doesn't have to be scared either.

But she still doesn't look convinced, even with my trick. I reach out to touch her arm like my mom always does when she wants me to understand something complicated, but Abby steps out of the way before I can make contact. She jerks her thumb over her shoulder toward her house.

"I gotta get home," she says, backing away. "I'll text you later?"

I open my mouth to ask what's wrong, or if she wants to talk more about practice, but she's leaping back over the fence before I even get a chance to say good-bye.

13

Traditions are like laws

only more fun. And waiting for Abby after gymnastics practice on Sunday mornings is one of my favorite traditions of all time.

Abby practices on Sundays, and most days after school. During the summer, she was in the gym every day except for the week we went to sleepaway camp. She said she had to be if she wanted any chance of ever being in the Olympics. At our age, a lot of gymnasts switch to homeschool so they have more time to practice, apparently. I didn't like the sound of that. Homeschool would mean less time for us to see each other. I know it's selfish, but I just don't think I could give that up.

Not that it matters, though. Because Abby is sticking with

Sunday mornings, and the routine of showing up at the gym and reading a new comic while I wait for her is pretty perfect.

I finish the Miles Morales graphic novel I checked out from the library yesterday, and there's still fifteen minutes left of practice. The sun is shining extra hard on me where I'm sitting outside of the gym, so I decide to dip my head inside to take a peek at practice. I usually don't come into the waiting area, so when I go in, Gretchen, the lady who runs the front desk, claps her hands as if I've just announced a new holiday specifically for women with curly red hair and bright green lipstick like her.

"Well, would you look at what we have here!" She presses a kiss to my cheek over the desk, and I can feel the sticky lipstick print she leaves behind. I smile anyway, though, because she's always so nice. "How are you? How's your mother? Is she still at the bakery? How *does* she get those scones to be so perfect every time? My word, they're delicious! Are you all still living over there on Arbor Way?"

Gretchen always talks so fast you almost have to take notes to keep up, but I've had some practice, so I rattle off my answers with ultra-speed—"Good. Great. Yes. Lots of practice. Yup, twelve years and counting. Bye!"—before ducking into the gym where Abby practices.

Inside looks a lot like a warehouse-sized playground, only much more complicated. There are a bunch of colored mats, and beams and bars, and even a foam pit to practice flipping into. I've never wanted to be a gymnast or anything, but I've always loved coming here to watch Abby. The way she moves through the air as though gravity is more of a suggestion than a reality, the way she has to have these absolutely out-of-this-world muscles to do stunts that make her way tougher than any boy our age—it's amazing.

She just barely missed qualifying for Junior Nationals last year, but she's gonna get gold this year. Obviously.

I spot Abby across the gym and don't wave right away. She's on a beam, and besides, I kind of want to surprise her and see the look on her face when she spots me. This is her least favorite event, so I watch her face get tight with focus before she leans back and swings her legs over her body twice before pushing off the beam and into the air for a flip. But she loses her balance, and instead of landing on her feet, she hits the mat on her back with a thud.

I want to run to her, but I know her coaches are better at helping her up than I am, so when I see her sit up and shake herself off, I decide not to wait in the gym after all.

Ten minutes later, Abby walks out of the locker room area with her gym bag over her shoulder. Her face is red and sweaty, and she doesn't smile when she sees me, not like usual. She looks pinched, like she's holding in a big burp.

She doesn't even stop when she reaches me. She just marches straight out to the parking lot.

"Abby, wait!" I wave good-bye to Gretchen as I run out to catch up with Abby. She's being so weird. "Where's the fire?"

I think of all the reasons she might be upset, but I can't come up with anything. Is she embarrassed because I saw her fall? That would be silly. I've seen her fall hundreds of times. It's how we met, after all. Besides, Abby always says that the mark of a good gymnast isn't never falling, it's always getting back up. Which she did.

But she doesn't answer right away and keeps looking forward when I catch up to her.

"Are you— Are you ignoring me?" I move to stand in front of her and make my voice peppier than I feel. "What's the matter? We always meet up after practice."

She crosses her arms and looks up at the sky. "Nothing is the matter."

"Okayyyyyy." I drag out the word. "So why are you marching down Main like a toy soldier?"

"Did you have to come inside?" she blurts out. "Maybe I don't want you to see me—"

Fall? I wonder, and then my eyes get all buggy with surprise. Coming inside the gym has never been a problem before, and neither has seeing her not land a trick. It's just part of the sport. I don't understand.

"I just mean—" she goes on. "We don't have to do everything together, right? Like, maybe the gym should be off-limits on practice days for you. And . . . and Wrigley's can be off-limits for me."

The way my mouth opens and closes, and no words come

out, I must look like Burt the Betta Fish. But I'm so confused. My chest feels like all the air has been sucked out of my lungs. Me and Abby have never fought and have never, *ever* had off-limits zones for our friendship. What's hers is mine and what's mine is hers, down to the time we had to share a toothbrush on the last day of camp when she accidentally dropped hers in the toilet. See, we've even shared our plaque!

I don't want to agree. I don't care whether she comes to the comic book store with me or not. But *she* cares if I come to the gym, and that's what matters. That's what she's saying.

"I have to go," she says after a second of us standing there staring at each other. "I'm supposed to meet Marley at the mall later."

She uncrosses her arms and wraps them around my shoulders. I don't hug back right away, but she squeezes me anyway.

"Look, I'm just freaking out, El. This is kind of intense, you know? With ... everything."

She waves her hand up and down my body, and I know right away what she means. How could I have forgotten, even for a second, that Abby still hasn't figured out how to deal with the fact that her best friend is a freak of nature? I feel like each one of her words is a bucket of water being dropped on my head. All sorts of questions start to bubble up inside me at once.

All Abby talks about is wanting to make her mark, so shouldn't she want the same for me? What if my powers are the thing I'm supposed to bring to the world?

What if I'm not supposed to hide them at all?

"I'm sorry. Ignore me." She steps back and hikes her gym bag higher on her shoulder. "I'll come over when I'm done at the mall, okay? Maybe we can watch one of your movies together or something."

I try to convince myself that she sounds at least a little bit excited about the idea of hanging out, but I know her voice better than my own. That's the same way she sounds when she tells her mom, *I'll get to the dishes after I finish painting my nails, okay?*

We walk side by side all the way back to our street, but I don't remember anything I said the whole way. It's a fifteen-minute walk, but it feels like it takes hours. Every step feels wrong-footed, like I'm wearing a pair of shoes that are about four sizes too small. I thought my powers were the biggest change in the world, but maybe I was wrong.

And I have no idea what to do about it.

I don't like being a spy

but I am a very good one. So, even though this isn't the way I wanted to spend my Saturday afternoon, the first thing I do after Abby disappears into the Ortega house is run upstairs and dig through my closet for spy-appropriate clothes. I'm gonna follow her to the mall, and I'm gonna figure out exactly what's so great about Marley Keilor other than her perfect ponytail and shiny-glossy lips and expensive clothes.

Well. Okay. That's a lot of good stuff. But not enough good stuff to abandon your best friend over!

"No, nope, not that, *definitely* not that." I reject everything I have for being too obvious. Ugh.

Abby knows all my clothes, which means I don't have that

many options. But Mom is working, and the house is empty, so her closet is available for digging!

I dash across the hallway and dip into my mom's room. It's super clean, as usual, and the closet door is shut neatly, no clothes exploded all over the hangers and door and floor like in my room. I open it up, and on the floor, in the back, there's a box of stuff my dad accidentally left behind when he moved out. My mom thinks I don't know about it, but I do.

I only ever touch it when I'm feeling really sad, or missing him more than usual, but these are desperate times and this is a very, *very* desperate measure.

I dig out a hoodie that used to fit my dad's giant body, pull it on, and zip it up to my neck. It goes all the way down to my knees and looks more like I'm wearing a trash bag with a hood than clothes. I borrow a pair of my mom's big, round, beetle-eye sunglasses, and check myself out in the mirror. No way Abby will recognize me in this.

My mom doesn't like for me to ride my bike too far from the house without permission, but the mall is at least fifteen minutes away by bike, which definitely counts as *too far*.

"No risk, no reward," I say under my breath as I roll my bike out of the garage. "I'll just have to be quick, I guess."

I sneak my bike across the backyard so the Ortegas won't see me riding down our street. Once I hit Sycamore, I pedal like my life depends on it in the direction of the mall. I'm huffing and puffing the entire ride and sweating buckets inside the baggy old hoodie I'm wearing. Also, the sunglasses are too big, so they keep slipping down my sweaty nose and making it hard to see. I almost hop the curb and take out an old lady walking her little wiener dog trying to push the glasses back up my face.

It is the worst, messiest, most exhausting bike ride I've ever taken.

By the time I get to the mall and lock my bike to the rack, I almost think this might not have been a good idea. But then I hear Abby's voice across the parking lot, and Marley's stupid little giggle to match, and know that this is the only way.

They're still far away enough that I don't think they can see me, but I drop down behind the row of bushes lining the front walkway just in case. There's a branch poking me in my side and I'm pretty sure there's an ant crawling up my leg that makes me wanna stop drop and roll. But Abby's lavender shampoo hits my nose at the same time as her floppy sandals slap against the sidewalk right in front of me, so I don't move a muscle and—yup, that's definitely an ant.

Ew, oh yuck, oh my gosh ew. I hop up and do a little dance to get the bugs and twigs off me as soon as Abby and Marley are out of sight. And then, the mission commences.

I power walk inside, trying to keep a stealthy distance from Abby and Marley. Anytime they stop to look at one of the booths that line the middle of the mall walkways, I spin so my back is to them and pretend to be super interested in whatever's in front of me. Marley stops to look at a jewelry stand, and I turn my head so fast my neck practically cracks.

"Hey, dude, can I help you find anything?" the guy at the cell-phone-charger booth asks when I stop. I pretend to be super interested in a twenty-foot charge cord that supposedly doubles as a satellite radio beacon, and lower my voice to sound like one of the boys in my class.

"No, um, bro." I cough. "Man, I'm good, dude. You got the new PS5? Uh, football game?"

Nailed it.

The guy's face screws up in confusion at the same time Marley and Abby start moving again, so I hike my hood higher and offer a quick "Thanks, uh, brother?" and keep walking.

I shove my hands into my pockets and hunch my shoulders to be more inconspicuous as I trail them from as far back as I can without losing their voices.

"Oh my *gawd*, he's staring—he's totally staring!" I hear Marley whisper-shout.

She and Abby are strolling arm in arm and stop suddenly outside American Eagle. For a second, I think Marley's talking about me, and I pat myself on the back for having such a convincing disguise that Marley thinks I'm a cute boy, but then I realize she's not talking about me at all. She's looking at my curly-headed, angel-faced, sworn nemesis.

It's Sammy Spencer.

I squat down behind the flavored popcorn stand and scoot

out just enough so that I can see what's going on. My powers don't give me X-ray vision, which I realize now would have been a really great help in a moment like this. Super-smell? Useless. Being able to see your new sworn enemy and your traitorous best friend through a glass case full of cheddar-cheese popcorn? Priceless.

It's harder than I thought to hear over everything else going on in the mall. I can hear the dishes clanging in the food court kitchens, the registers cha-chinging in every store. I can even smell the other cinnamon pretzel booth all the way on the opposite end of the mall, and my mouth starts watering automatically. It's overwhelming, and a little scary, but also kind of cool. Or it would be cool, maybe, if my ability to sense all those other things didn't also mean that I had to sneak around after my best friend, or crawl behind the giant potted plant in the food court to get a better look at her and Marley when they move closer to the window.

The big leaves of the plant are all brownish and spotted with holes instead of being full and vibrant green like they're supposed to be, and I realize that if Abby or Marley turns around, I'm toast. These leaves aren't hiding anything.

"See, Ellie, this is why you should be the seeker and not the hider," I mumble. Without stopping to overthink it, I dig my fingers into the soil near my face until I can feel some of the thin roots, and the leaves snap back to their full form, sheltering me from view.

"He's so cute!" Abby covers her face with her hands, but I can still see her blushing. Sammy is inside looking at jeans, and Abby and Marley watch through the window of the store. "He's definitely the cutest boy ever, right?"

"Oh yeah. Definitely."

For a second, I think Marley's being awfully obvious and Sammy's definitely gonna notice her, and then I remember that her voice only sounds like a gunshot to me, not everyone in the mall. Well, her voice sounds like a cheese grater against a chalkboard, so it's probably pretty bad to everyone else, too. Just not for the same reasons.

I don't have to strain to hear Abby, either, but I almost wish I did.

"Ellie doesn't think so," she says quietly. "She just . . . doesn't get it."

Abby thinks I don't get her anymore?

The air feels like it got sucked out of my lungs. Suddenly, I wish I hadn't come. I should have just stayed home with Burt the Betta Fish and read or watched TV or done my homework. Anything would have been better than this. My whole life, Abby has known everything about me, and I've known everything about her. But Marley comes along, and I become some not-so-super hero, and now me not having crushes on boys is just another thing that makes me and Abby too different, I guess.

It's another thing I can't help that I wish I could.

"What does she know?" Marley says in a voice that sounds like she's laughing.

I try to hear what Abby says in return, but all of a sudden, a set of feet get caught in my extra-big hoodie fabric and I'm squashed under a pile of flailing arms and legs and spitting a handful of spilled cheddar-cheese popcorn out of my mouth.

"Oof!" the person sprawled over my back shouts, their boots way too close to kicking me in my nose.

All of the fancy mall popcorn (that didn't end up in my mouth) is scattered all over the floor, and a bunch of sticky-faced little kids marching out of the arcade point in our direction and laugh. Ugh. Just when you think dressing up in spy gear to snoop on your best friend from behind an oversized potted plant couldn't get any more embarrassing, some third graders come along and remind you that being older absolutely does *not* make you cooler.

"What the heck?" I grisper—a word I make up specifically for this new experience of groaning and whispering at the same time. I scramble to sit up, still attempting to stay hidden behind the plant. I try to will myself to disappear, but it's too late. I've been caught. "What are you—"

"Ellie?" Breonna's face is suddenly level with mine, her big brown eyes confused and her puff full of popcorn kernels as she whispers, "There's a bench you could sit on right over there! What are you doing down here?"

I'm tempted to slap a hand over her mouth just in case Abby

or Marley discovers us, but I manage to keep my cool and come up with a really good cover story instead.

"Ummmmmm." I gulp. "I have a new job doing floor inspections?"

*

I've been a Nosy Parker my whole life, even before the super-senses kicked in. I was really good at hearing things I wasn't supposed to hear when I was younger. It's why my mom used to call me a Nosy Parker.

I don't know who Nosy Parker is, but the context clued me in to the fact that they were probably a big pain in the neck. I didn't mean to be nosy, though. I just always happened to be at interesting places at interesting times. And because I was quiet, no one noticed me there until they'd already started spilling their guts.

One time, I was reading a graphic novel underneath the counter of the bakery and Poppy stubbed his toe so hard against a chair, he used a word that meant he owed the swear jar a dollar and he thought nobody noticed. But when I popped out for money collection, he used it again *and* said I was gonna give him a heart attack. Another time, Mom was on the phone with my aunt Tasha in the kitchen while I was in the cupboard looking for snacks and said that her and my dad were just "a square peg in a round hole."

I didn't know what it meant then, but when I accidentally knocked over the cereal shelf and she noticed me in there, her hand shot up to cover her mouth, and I knew it was nothing good. A few months later, Burt the Betta Fish was swimming around in his bowl, and my dad was driving a moving van all the way to Arizona.

I tried extra hard not to hear anything I wasn't supposed to from then on.

I don't know why I tell Bree any of this, but I do. I explain that I was snooping, but not why. I can't tell her about my powers or how I think girls are cuter than boys or that I think I'm losing my best friend without feeling embarrassed or maybe even putting her in danger—at least with the powers thing—but it's good to say some of it out loud. Especially to someone like Bree, who's so good at listening.

We're sitting in the food court, and I've shoved my sunglasses and big hoodie into a shopping bag so I don't look as weird. She takes a sip from her straw that's stuck in the Bahama Mama smoothie we're sharing and slides it back over to me so I can take one, too. She doesn't say anything right away, but I know it's because she's thinking, not because she doesn't care.

"You must miss your dad," she finally says.

"Yeah." I nod and take a sip. "I mean, my mom said that endings can also be new beginnings, but. I don't know. I wish his new beginning hadn't had to happen without me."

"I get it. Sort of." She balls up her straw wrapper and rolls it between her fingers. "My big brother went to college last year, and he's only been home once since. I know he's supposed to grow up and get his own life, but it still sucks."

I didn't know Bree had an older brother. And then I realize, there's a lot I don't know about her. There's a lot I don't know about most of my classmates. For a long time, the sun, moon, and the stars has been Abby, and I know—*knew*—her better than I knew anything other than comic books. But while I was focused on that person, a lot has been happening around me that I've missed.

"You think there's a potion or something to make the suck ever stop sucking?" I ask.

She takes the last sip of our smoothie and smiles. "No. But do you promise to text each other the second we figure it out?" She holds up her pinkie for me to swear on. "We'll make note of it for scientific purposes. Become rich and famous. Never have to sit in classes with people like Marley again."

I laugh and link my pinkie through hers. It's one of the easiest promises I've ever made.

I'm so bored I could puke

on Monday when Abby decides to stay late at cheerleading practice instead of coming over to do homework together like usual, and my mom picks up some extra students to tutor. SAT season is here and the high schooler parents on the other side of town are starting to freak out about their kids getting into Harvard or whatever, so when I get home from school, I see a note on the fridge saying that she might be a little late for dinner and that I should heat up some frozen nuggets in the microwave in case I get hungry.

We're only one day in, but I'm already wishing for the week to be over. Maybe even the school year. It's not off to the best start.

Abby didn't discover me at the mall, but that didn't make today any less awkward. At lunch, she kept looking over at the cheerleading girls like she couldn't imagine anything better than going over to sit with them, and I couldn't stop thinking about what she'd said in the store about me not understanding her. It was awkward, but neither of us wanted to say as much.

It reminds me of this lesson on magnetic poles we got in science last week. Opposite ends of a magnet attract each other, but the same ends push each other away. I wish we were more like magnets. Then maybe our oppositeness would bring us closer together rather than push us apart.

Now I pluck Mom's note from the fridge and tuck it into my pocket with a sigh. I check in on Burt the Betta Fish in his bowl on the floor of my room, hidden between my bedside table and the wall, where Mom wouldn't find it unless she was really searching.

"What's up, buddy?" I lie down on the carpet, and he swims toward the glass to greet me, his bright orange tail whipping around like a tiny hairless golden retriever. "Yeah, I missed you, too."

I sprinkle a little food on the surface, and he pecks at it with Thanksgiving-dinner happiness. He has no idea that he saw the light and then got jolted back to life in a way that defies the laws of space and time. But then again, I'm not sure he has an idea about much of anything, considering his brain is the size of a pinhole.

"It's been a while since it was just the two of us, huh?" I sprinkle in a little more food. "Weird."

For a long time, it's been me *and.* Me and Abby watching old movies on her family's ancient DVD player. Me and Mom counting out our coupons for Sunday-morning grocery shopping. Me and Poppy arguing about the best Marvel villain. Today, it's just me and my trusty half-zombie pet Betta fish. And I hate the way it feels.

So I go down to the garage, pull the old paint sheet off my bike, and hop on. I shrug on my backpack and kick up the stand. There aren't many places I can go without Mom's permission, but moving feels better than standing still. And as long as I'm riding, I might be able to out-pedal the quiet. I don't stop pedaling until I get to Wrigley's. I hop off my bike and lean it up against the building's brick wall before walking in. Inside, I breathe deep and take in the scent of old matte paper and the dusty memorabilia that Kyle, the guy at the counter, never bothers to clean.

I feel at home.

I don't know who Wrigley is, or why he gave his comic book shop such a boring name, but I probably owe him a couple hundred thank-yous. Wrigley's Comics is my absolute favorite place in Plainsboro. It's got so many rows of comic books and DVDs and memorabilia that you could spend hours inside and still not see everything.

Poppy used to bring me here every Saturday morning

before walking me over to meet Abby after gymnastics. Mom was never into comics, and Poppy didn't talk about them with Dad, either. To be honest, Poppy didn't like him, even before my parents split up ("I don't trust no man who don't wash his apples before eating them. It just ain't God's way!" he once admitted after Dad moved out). But me? I was sold the first time Poppy handed me a comic in a plastic sleeve in kindergarten.

"Just because you can't read yet ain't an excuse not to be well-read," he'd said. "Here's some fine literature." He took the coloring book out of my hand and shoved in a copy of *Justice League of America*. "The Bible says train up a child in the way they should go, and I'll be darned if you aren't trained up right."

Everything was possible in comic books, he told me. The Big Bads got defeated—most of the time—and truth and justice always prevailed.

"It's better than the real world that way." He tapped the page where it lay open in front of me.

I ran my hands over the soft paper until I pieced the stories together from the pictures. I wasn't always right, of course. But it was always fun.

"In here, things make sense," Poppy went on. "Up is up, down is down, and the guy—or lady, I ain't discriminating!—in the cape usually wins."

I thought about the picture of Poppy and Mr. Walker in their army uniforms that hung on the bakery wall.

"You didn't have a cape on when you went to fight the bad guys, Poppy. And you're still one of the good guys," I said.

Poppy shook his head and sighed. He got that look that Mr. Walker had all the time—the one where his eyes seemed to be looking at everything and nothing at the same time. I didn't like that look very much.

"That's what I mean about the real world, kid. It's more complicated than that," he said after a while. "The good guys ain't always so good, and the bad guys ain't always so bad."

When I'm at Wrigley's, I feel like Poppy is around me. We're lying on the floor of the living room while he tells me some story about his life before he met Gramma Candy. When he was what he called a young buck without two nickels to rub together, and Mr. Walker was the funniest guy on the block.

And now it feels so good to flip through an old issue of *Superman: Son of Kal El* and think about Jon Kent—Clark Kent and Lois Lane's son—and his almost-limitless powers that I don't even notice that there's a person next to me until Sammy Spencer says, "Oh man, people were so mad about that one."

My body goes stiff as a board, and I think about running back outside. I've never run into anybody from school at Wrigley's before, and I'm not really sure what to do. This isn't the kind of place I go to socialize. I come here to get lost in all the worlds that are so much bigger and more exciting than Plainsboro. And on days like today, I come here to forget about how complicated everything outside of these four walls is. Including the power that I can feel thrumming just under my fingertips.

I drop the comic and shove my hands into my pockets on instinct. Like if Sammy looks hard enough at them he might know everything there is to know about how much of a freak I am.

"Sorry," Sammy says, his voice actually sounding apologetic. He picks up the comic and lays it on the table in front of me without batting an eye. "I didn't mean to scare you. That's just a really wild issue."

Issue #5 of *Superman: Son of Kal-El* is the one where Jon Kent comes out as bisexual. When it was announced, people online hated it and said really terrible things about the fact that no son of Superman—no *real* superhero—could possibly be anything other than straight. But when I heard about it, I took the few dollars Mr. Walker had given me to sweep up the shop and walked straight to Wrigley's. I read the entire issue right in the middle of the store. It was amazing. I never thought a hero could be like me. Or sort of like me, at least.

Of course Sammy would think it was "wild." He wouldn't get it.

"What's so wild about it?"

I turn to give him the evil eye. I've been practicing that look a lot lately. Just in case it turns out that I fall more on the villain side of things than the hero side. Can't be too safe.

"Oh, just how weird people were about having a bi Superman

like it's a big deal or something." Sammy shakes his head, and his curls fall into his eyes. "My moms thought it was the best thing ever. They bought, like, ten copies just because."

I stare at Sammy while he flips through the rack of comics in front of him like he didn't just say the biggest, most unexpected thing ever.

"You have two moms?" I ask.

"Yeah!" He smiles in a happy-lopsided way. He leans back against the rack and jerks his thumb over his shoulder. "That's my Mama Lottie by the register. She's the one who loves anime and comic books and stuff."

I look over his shoulder and see his mom giving some money to the cashier. She has jet-black hair that stops at her shoulders and colorful tattoos winding all the way up her arm. She's even wearing a pair of Converse with the Green Lantern logo painted on the side. I'm pretty sure she's the coolest adult I've ever seen.

I had no idea anyone in Plainsboro had two moms. And I definitely didn't think someone like Sammy, who is the most popular guy in school and never gets made fun of for anything, ever, would have two moms. My whole brain just got scrambled like eggs right in the middle of the comic book store.

"That's, um, that's really—" *Don't say anything embarrassing, Ellie!* "Normal. Really regular and normal that you have two moms and one of them likes comic books. Um. Yeah."

Very smooth.

Sammy's cheeks get a little pink, but he doesn't stop smiling. He opens his mouth to say something, but right then, his mom grabs her receipt and waves at the both of us. I wave back at her, and Sammy sighs.

"Guess I gotta go," he says. "But I'll see you in science tomorrow, right?"

I nod and Sammy shuffles toward the exit. His mom ruffles his hair as she holds the door open for him to walk through. I can't believe I had a conversation with Sammy Spencer. And not just any conversation, but one about one of my favorite comic book runs, which he also likes, and his super-cool moms. It's all so weird that I don't have room in my brain to think about anything else. I'm not sad or lonely or intimidated by my powers in that moment. I'm just kind of happy.

That happiness carries me all the way up to the register, and before I leave, I buy another copy of issue #5 just because.

*

All I can think about is meatballs the entire way home from my bike ride.

I know they're on the menu for dinner tonight, and I can't wait. My mom doesn't make them from scratch or anything—they're the freezer kind you have to cook in the microwave—but she does something fancy with the tomato sauce that makes it taste like barbecue sauce, and it's my absolute favorite meal.

My mouth is pretty much watering by the time I drop my bike in the driveway next to Mom's car.

But I can hear shouting coming from next door as easily as if it were a song playing through my headphones, and I take a step toward the Ortegas'. It's not like they have a perfect family or anything—I know there's no such thing—but the Ortegas hardly ever fight. When my mom and dad got divorced, Abby didn't really understand how it could have happened. It didn't make sense to her that the two people who had made a promise to love each other for always could one day decide they didn't love each other at all. But I knew how easy it was, even if she didn't.

"You can't just walk away! After everything we've done to get here?" Mrs. Ortega's voice sounds sharp enough to break glass, and I bring my shoulders up to my ears like that'll be enough to muffle it.

I want to text Abby and check in on her, give her some advice from an old pro, and then I realize that Mr. and Mrs. Ortega aren't yelling at each other. Mrs. Ortega is yelling at *Abby*.

Abby, who cleans her room without being asked. Abby, who always eats her vegetables at dinner even though she says cauliflower tastes like broccoli that gave up on life. Abby, who *never* gets in trouble.

Abby storms out the front door and slams it behind her. She's still wearing her purple-and-white Easton Junior High

Seventh Grade Cheer T-shirt and black shorts from practice. I can hear her mom still shouting inside, even though Abby is now sitting on the porch. I don't even hesitate before cutting across both of our yards to sit down next to her.

I don't think about how I felt when she ditched me for her new friends the other day until she tucks her knees up to her chest, wraps her arms around them, and without even looking at me says, "I bet you heard everything."

Her voice sounds even worse than sad—it sounds like nothing. Like someone has squished her words down to squeeze any emotion out of them.

I cross my arms over my knees. Except for the recon mission at the mall, if I could avoid hearing stuff I'm not supposed to hear, I would. She should know that.

I mumble, "I just got home. I only heard yelling. Not what it was about."

She presses her lips together and looks in the opposite direction, like she doesn't want me to see she's crying. I try not to let that hurt my feelings. I've seen Abby cry at least a million times in our lives. About everything from the Willa Moon and Cal Key breakup to coming in second behind Bethany on the balance beam at a meet two months ago. Abby wipes at her eyes with the back of her hand, smearing the thick black mascara she's been wearing for school the past couple of days. I saw Marley applying the same kind to her eyelashes in Language Arts.

I press my shoulder against hers and wait. Sometimes that's all you can do with Abby. She's loud, and bold, and definitely a little brash, but when she gets like this, all that disappears.

"I quit gymnastics today."

I know there's zero percent chance I misheard her, but I can't really understand the words. Abby without gymnastics? It's like a peanut butter sandwich without bananas—unheard of.

"What?"

"I don't want to do it anymore, El. I'm not—" She snorts up her snot and looks at me. "I'll never look like Bethany." She holds up her pinkie and shakes her head. "And it's not fun for me anymore, always comparing myself to the other girls. I just wanna cheer."

I look down at her and try to grasp what she's talking about. Over the summer she had a growth spurt, one that skipped me altogether. Abby wears a bra every day now. And not those training bras we bought together in fourth grade because we wanted to be more grown up—the real thing, from the PINK store in the mall. And, the day before her birthday last December, she also started her period. Abby had been hit full force with the birds-and-the-bees stuff they warned us about in fifth grade health. But it hadn't made her any less powerful, or beautiful. Because the stuff that made Abby *Abby* wasn't about her body.

My heart starts beating too fast when I think about how going to the pool with her this summer was different from all the summers before. It was like overnight I wasn't the only person who knew how amazing she was. All of a sudden, boys were staring in our direction while we put on sunscreen, and I knew exactly why. As we waited in line for the two-person water slide or the low diving board, I'd heard whispers about the "thick Ortega girl." But none of that mattered to me. Because I knew the most important things about Abby—that she was funny, and a little weird, and she'd been my best friend since kindergarten.

"Abby…"

I don't know what to say. Since we were six, all Abby has ever wanted was to go to the Olympics. To be only the fifth Latina gymnast ever to be on Team USA. To make her mark. But if this isn't her dream anymore, then she'll find another one. And I'll applaud her on from the sidelines of that dream, too.

"At least now we'll have more time to spend together?" I say, trying to sound hopeful.

"Yeah, maybe," she says. She twirls the ends of her ponytail around her finger. "But I'm thinking of doing some extra practices with some girls from cheer now, too. To show my mom that I'm really serious about it, you know?"

My heart feels like it's been opened, and not in a good, happy, emotions-leaking-all-over-the-place kind of way. That means I'll probably see even less of Abby. It means that the way I felt earlier before going to the comic book store might happen more and more often. But Poppy said that loving people was about putting their needs first sometimes. And there's a lot I don't know, but I know I love Abby. So I try to patch over the hole in my heart fast.

"You'll be the best one on the cheer team," I finally say, smiling. "Better at cheer than Bethany is at gymnastics, for sure."

Abby's head shoots up from where it's been lying on her knees. A wobbly smile breaks across her face.

"You really think?"

"What kind of question is that? It's like asking if Batman is really from Gotham City."

Abby rolls her eyes. "Okay, well, I don't know the answer to that one, either, weirdo."

"Yes." I laugh. I throw my arm around her, and she rests her head on my shoulder. For a second, everything feels right. Me and Abby together. Me and Abby supporting each other. Me and Abby laughing about her complete lack of comic book knowledge. It's perfect. "Batman is definitely from Gotham, and you're definitely gonna kill it on the cheer team. Both are facts."

Mrs. Ortega comes out a few minutes later to call Abby in for dinner, and I give my friend's shoulder one more squeeze before I run to my house. When I get inside, the meatballs are on the stove, and the TV is on in the other room. There's a comic book in my backpack, picked out with some help from an unexpectedly cool Sammy Spencer. I can feel the gentle thrum of my powers in my hands, but I haven't had any incidents with them in days. Burt the Betta Fish is swimming upstairs, Mom is home for the night, and from the sound of it, she's still awake.

"Belly, pop your dinner in the microwave and come in here with me!" she yells from the living room. "Netflix added a new Denzel Washington movie this weekend, and you know how I feel about Denzel."

My phone has a text from Abby that says: **ily forever bestie**

I reply the way we always have: **forever and two days**

Life's good.

16

Nothing is worse than a roomful of know-it-alls

getting ready to do an experiment where they have to cut open a thing that used to be alive. The minute we put on our lab goggles and plastic aprons, every seventh grader in Advanced Science becomes Bruce Banner Junior.

"You're not doing it right!"

"No, *this* is how the pins go into the arm. See?"

"You're gonna puke all over everything—move!"

The kids in this science class are the ones who were on the "advanced track" in elementary. That's a fancy way of saying our class is full of honor-roll goody-goodies. People like Marley Keilor, who get straight As but are mostly smart about terrible things. Like how you can make people cry the fastest when something embarrassing happens to them. For example, when someone bleeds through their pants during tug-of-war at summer camp because they got their period for the first time and you call them the Creature from the Blood Lagoon in front of your entire cabin.

Not that I know anyone that happened to or anything. Obviously.

Advanced also means we get to do cool stuff earlier than the rest of the kids in our grade. Stuff like dissecting frogs. It's kind of disgusting to think about—poking around inside an innocent amphibian—but it's also pretty cool. We spent all last year studying cells and organs to prepare for this experiment. The worksheets and the homework were the boring part, but this is the bright light at the end of the tunnel.

Everyone in the room is all hopped up on the experiment, in good ways and bad, with some reviewing their textbooks, some rubbing their hands together like evil villains, and others pretending to throw up from the smell of the stuff they use to keep the frogs from looking even more gross than they already do. Even Sammy Spencer is into it.

I know I saw him just yesterday at Wrigley's, and it wasn't totally awful. But there's something about being back in school and knowing that Marley is staring in our direction like a hawk just to get a better view of Sammy's sparkly eyes or whatever, that makes it hard to talk to him like I would anybody else. In a comic, a character who has no allegiance to either the good guys or the bad guys is called true neutral. Wrigley's is kind of like that. There are no sides in a comic book store. Just people and our imaginations.

School isn't like that, though. There are sides, and people like Marley and Sammy are on one end, and people like me and Bree are on the other. Even now, Sammy somehow still manages to look like he belongs on TV in the big, goofy lab goggles that we're required to wear for the dissection. Meanwhile, I'm pretty sure I look like a supremely uncool version of Cyclops.

"I'm not really sure where to start." Sammy squints at the instructions printout we got when we came in and takes notes on the back of it. At least if he were a bad lab partner, I could be annoyed at him for that, but he won't even slack off like I want him to! He's the *worst*. "This whole thing is kind of creepy."

Tell me about it, I want to say. But then I think about how he's all Abby has wanted to talk about besides cheer since the beginning of the school year—how cute and sweet and *perfect* he is—and I just shrug instead. I'm not gonna give him the satisfaction of being another member of his fan club.

"So do you want to do the honors or should I?"

He points at the pins on the tabletop. We're supposed to stick them in the frog to keep the body from moving around while we work. He smiles and when he does, his nose crinkles a little, which makes him look like a kid in a candy store. Ugh.

All last night I practiced what I would say today to get out of having to do any of the actual dissecting. We're supposed to put on those plastic hospital gloves before we start, but even so I didn't want to accidentally touch the frog and then, you know. Presto chango, tap-dancing frog, ruined life. The whole thing.

"I have, uh, um"—*Okay, Ellie, make it convincing! Just like we rehearsed it!*—"moral resistance to being a part of any form of animal cruelty."

I know my words make me sound like a robot, even though I went over those lines like a hundred times. I stole them from the episode of Willa Moon's reality show where she said she only ate GMO-free, organic, vegan, gluten-free, paraben-free, sun-dried kale breakfast smoothies because of her new religion.

In real life, I feel kind of sad for the frog, I guess. I mean, he didn't deserve to die just so a bunch of seventh graders could poke around in his insides. But I'm mostly excited to be learning something new. Even if I can't actually do much besides write our answers on the worksheet.

"Oh," Sammy says. He looks surprised as he shakes his curls out of his eyes. "That's cool. My grandpa always says a man should have a strong value system. But that goes for every gender, right? I can do the cutting part."

He smiles like he really means it, with his dimples and rosy-red cheeks, so I start smiling, too.

"Yeah." I nod. I can sort of get why people think he's cool.

But Abby still has big heart-eyes every time his name comes up, so I force my mouth into a straight line to look extra serious. "Okay."

"Sammy-Boo!"

Marley leans against our table with her phone in her hand stretched out far enough to get Sammy and her in the camera together. I roll my eyes so hard it hurts. Leave it to Marley to try and livestream a video of a frog dissection to her few hundred followers just to get some extra likes. If I were a tattletale, I'd be ratting her out for using her phone right now even though it's against Mrs. Morales's lab rules. But I'm no snitch—even if watching Marley Keilor get detention would be like my own personal Christmas.

"Uh, hey, Marley." Sammy pushes his goggles up the bridge of his nose and, unlike Marley, actually seems a little freaked out about having a camera in his face at a moment like this. He even blushes. "What's up?"

"I just wanted my followers to see how *adorable* you looked in your scientist outfit!"

Sammy looks down at his outfit and shrugs. He's wearing checkered Vans, jeans, and a white-and-blue tie-dyed hoodie. If this is what scientists look like, then Bruce Banner seriously has the wrong idea about fashion.

"Marley!" Mrs. Morales turns around from the lab table where she's helping another pair pin their frog and jerks her head toward the area where Marley is supposed to be.

"Going, Mrs. M." Marley smiles and blows a kiss at Sammy as she leaves. She doesn't even bother to put her phone away when she gets back to her lab table and mumbles to her partner, "It's totally unfair that *she* gets to be partners with Sammy. She doesn't even seem happy to be there. I heard she doesn't even think he's cute."

I'm not supposed to be able to hear her, but that doesn't make it any easier to listen to. Not that I care what Marley thinks of me—not that I care what *anyone* thinks of me, really, except my best friend—but what she's saying makes my neck hot and my stomach feel like someone is stirring my insides with a soup ladle.

Abby told her that, I think. *Abby told her that and now she's using it against me.*

Marley is talking into her phone now, not-so-subtly pointing it in our direction, and giggling. I'm not surprised. Marley is the type of person who gets joy out of making anyone who is different than her feel uncomfortable. And even without the powers, I know I'm different.

I've known it for a long time. But I'll never tell anyone why. Because the minute people know, nothing would be simple anymore. Everything would get even more complicated. My mom didn't sign up for a complicated daughter. She shouldn't have to deal with my messy feelings about Abby on top of everything else. Because no matter how I feel, I'm not like Sammy's moms, all bold and proud.

No, I don't want to be partners with Sammy. No, I don't have a crush on him like every other girl in our grade. No, I don't care about how cute or smart he is. Because I'm—

"I bet she's ga—"

"No!"

I have to stop her. I try to push past Sammy, as if I have any hope of getting to Marley's phone before she says it to everyone on her livestream. All I can think about is keeping her from blurting out my secret, the thing that, before I got my powers, was the biggest secret I'd ever had to keep. But at the same moment I dive toward Marley, Sammy pulls our dissection tray closer to himself so he can push in the first pin. My hand lands smack on top of the table and I stop.

Everything stops.

Because that wasn't the table at all. It's squishy and slimy, and now, *alive*.

"Oh my god!" Marley screams, pointing a finger and her camera at us. At *me*.

My heart stops beating just as another heart restarts.

The screams of everyone else in the room, and the happy throaty *ribbit* of our recently dead science experiment are the last things I hear before the entire world—and *my* entire world—turns upside down.

The world wasn't *technically* upside down

but I definitely was. When I wake up in the nurse's office, the kid on the cot next to me isn't even pretending not to stare directly at me. Manners. Seriously.

The boy has brown hair that's shaved close to his head and neon-yellow glasses with no lenses in them. Between the color and the haircut, he looks a little like a nosy tennis ball.

"Um," I say. I sit up and rub my eyes. People don't usually stare at me. I'm pretty good at blending in with the wallpaper. "Hi?"

The boy's jaw is practically dragging on the ground while he looks at me. And just like that, everything that happened before

I passed out hits me like a runaway train. Sammy's eyes bugging out of his head. Mrs. Morales praying the rosary. Marley Keilor smiling and screaming at the same time like someone just offered her an invitation to Willa Moon's exclusive birthday party on an island you can only get to by submarine.

"It's *you*," Tennis Ball Boy whispers. He points like I'm an animal behind a glass wall in the zoo and says even louder, "You're Frog Girl!"

I shake my head. This can't be happening. What am I gonna do about my mom? About *Abby*? And how am I gonna—

Wait. *Frog Girl?* No way that's my superhero name. Couldn't they have come up with something cooler if they were gonna ruin my life? I look up at the ceiling and groan. Today couldn't get any worse.

"Shh, no, that's not me. You've got the wrong person."

I swing my legs over the side of the cot and sit up. I can hear everything around me. Nurse Lee's Crocs squeak on the checkered floor as she paces back and forth on the other side of the curtain. They pretend like separating the beds from her desk gives you some privacy back here, but I can tell you from experience the curtain doesn't help much at all. When you slip into a panic attack so bad you faint in front of your entire science class after resurrecting a very dead, very oblivious frog on camera, a curtain can't really do much for your dignity.

"No, it's totally you! I watched the video!"

The boy reaches into his pocket and almost drops his phone

when he tries to shove it in my direction. I kind of wish he had dropped it. And cracked his screen. So he could never watch it again. That's my only plan at the moment: crack every phone screen in Plainsboro, and every laptop and tablet and smartwatch until there's no one who can watch the worst moment of my life on instant replay ever again.

Listen, I know the plan needs some work, okay? I didn't say it was perfect.

The video begins to play just as Nurse Lee starts talking on the phone. I try to focus on both things at once.

"Oh my god!" Marley screams behind the camera.

My face appears as Sammy backs away from me slowly, and I look like a ghost. Like someone just brought *me* back from the dead—my cheeks red, my eyes watering like I'm about to cry, my head shaking as if that would be enough to convince my classmates they didn't see what they saw. But it was plain as day: A frog was dead, and then I touched it—firmly touched it—and it came ribbiting back to life.

I paid attention to all the lessons about formaldehyde that we got before the dissection. It's pretty much like the frog had been given a shot that kept it from getting gross and shrivelly, but also made sure it was gone for good. In other words, that little frog should have been dead as a doornail. Gone with the wind. Not long for this world!

The only thing that could have brought him back to life was something bigger than science. It's pretty hard to deny, even though every bone in my body wants to. My powers must extend even further than I suspected they did if I can do something like this. I look down at my hands in my lap and try to stop them from shaking.

I'm in way deeper than I thought.

"Mrs. Engle, it's all very strange, but she's fine. I'm not sure I can explain it over the phone. Uh-huh," Nurse Lee whispers, all panicky-sounding.

I can hear my mom's voice on the other end. It's high-pitched like it gets when she's scared but trying not to show it. It's the same voice she had on parent-teacher night when she asked my kindergarten teacher what was wrong with me. It's the same voice she had the day she told me my dad was moving out but that didn't mean he didn't love me anymore. It's the voice I never, *ever* wanted to have to hear again.

On-screen, a girl I've never spoken to jumps onto a desk and starts crying, *"What's wrong with her? She touched it and it came back to life! She's a wizard!"* Someone else starts yelling, *"Don't touch her, she might be Jesus!"* while the undead frog leaps from the tray onto my head and makes a loud *ribbit!* from his perch on top of my one of my braids.

"I don't understand," my mom says. The sound of her keys jingling as she shoves one into the car's ignition fills the background. "But I'm on my way. Please tell her I'm on my way."

"This is gonna go so viral," Marley says on the video. Kids are shouting and knocking over chairs as she moves the camera

around the room. Some people are running as far away from me as they can get. Others are running toward me to get a better look at the freak show.

"Of course I will. See you very soon." Nurse Lee hangs up and pulls back the curtain.

I swallow around a lump in my throat as I watch what happens next. The frog jumps toward Marley and dives into the collar of her shirt. She drops her phone and screams as she tries to shake out the creature. My breath starts coming in too fast. There's not one eye in the room that isn't focused on me—on what I did. I pass out just as the live feed stops.

"Elliot?"

Nurse Lee calls me by my full name—the name that people only use when they don't really know me, or if things are really, *really* serious. Her heartbeat is so loud in my ears it takes everything in me to hear her voice over it. When she looks at me, she tries to be cool and collected like I bet they taught her in nurse school, but I can tell she's . . . scared. Like I'm a wild animal she has to put a collar on without getting her hand bitten off.

I hand the phone back to Tennis Ball Boy and sigh.

"Yes?"

Nurse Lee looks at the boy—who takes a quick picture of me without even bothering to turn off the click sound effect—and then back at me. She presses her lips together and shakes her head.

"Your mom is coming to pick you up." Her voice is gentle

even though I know how she really feels. What this means for her and for everyone who saw what I could do today.

How do you give medical help to someone who can bring a dead thing back to life with the accidental press of a finger? How do you treat a girl who can control what lives and dies without thinking twice about it? How do you go back to your everyday life knowing that the very thing you thought was most impossible is possible after all?

"Make sure to grab all your things. I don't think—"

She shakes her head again. She looks a little tired, a little confused. I get how she's feeling. My whole body feels like I've been in a boxing ring with the Hulk.

"I don't think you'll be coming back to school for a while."

18

I wish I'd paid more attention to Abby's gossipy magazines

because if I had, I might not be so caught off guard by the camera flashes bursting to my left and my right as me and Mom run up the front walkway and into our house. There's only a few people, and they look like they're from the local papers in the towns surrounding Plainsboro, but it's enough to leave spots dancing behind my eyes when I close them. I lock the door behind us quickly and lean back against it to take a breath. My mom rushes to pull the curtains closed while asking me question after question. I tried to explain things in the car, but she still doesn't get it.

Which, you know, fair. It's not every day your only daughter tells you she has the power to raise the dead.

"Explain it to me again."

My mom sits down at the kitchen table and leans forward. I flop down in the chair opposite her and immediately feel like I'm in one of those crime shows, with my mom playing the role of the friendly cop who's been pushed just a step too far by a suspect. There's no commercial break in sight.

Her eyeliner is all smudged because she's been rubbing at her eyes since she picked me up. I'm pretty sure she thinks she's stuck in a really horrible dream, and if she just blinks hard enough, she'll finally wake up.

"Mom..."

We've been over the story a hundred times by now, and it doesn't get any easier to tell or make any more sense with each explanation. But my mom likes recipes, she likes having instructions, she likes looking at a problem and coming up with answers. And I am the biggest problem of them all.

"Just humor me, please, okay?" Her phone buzzes on the table for the twentieth time in the past five minutes, and she reaches over to silence it. I bet it's the Xavier Institute calling to collect me. I'm doomed. "You woke up after the earthquake."

I nod.

"And you could *hear things*."

"Things I shouldn't have been able to hear. Yes."

"Like heartbeats."

I fold one of my hands on top of the other. And then I switch them. And when that doesn't keep them from buzzing, I shove them under my thighs.

"Like heartbeats," I repeat.

"And then you brought your fish back to life."

"Burt the Betta Fish."

She sighs. "Are you really correcting me about the zombie fish's full name right now, Elliot Leigh?"

"No, sorry." I drop my forehead onto the table with a thump. "Continue."

"And today you touched a dissection frog in science, and it started hopping around the room."

I groan in response. I don't look up, but I can feel her pull out the chair next to me at our small circular table and sit down. We don't use the table for eating anymore, not since Dad moved out. Most of the time we just eat in front of the TV, or, if Mom has had one of her really hard days, in her big bed. I never thought I'd miss the uncomfortable wooden chairs and the scratched-up tabletop, but . . . I miss a lot about how things used to be.

"Well, I always knew you were exceptional, Ellie-Belle." She squeezes the back of my neck with her soft hand, and I look up. She has a tired smile on her face. "But I have to admit, I never thought you were defy-the-laws-of-physics-and-biology exceptional."

Mom has always tried to make me believe I was something

special. Some*one* special. When I was little, she celebrated my every milestone like I'd just won the lottery. Learn to spell my name? Cupcakes for dinner. Get an A on a math quiz? We built a blanket fort in the living room and stuffed our faces with popcorn while watching scary movies that were off-limits any other time.

But what I liked best were the dance parties. I didn't do anything special for those. Sometimes, back when the bakery was her only job, Mom would pick me up from school, and the minute we walked through the front door she'd turn up the Bluetooth speaker on the counter and start blaring some old song. My favorite was called "Before I Let Go" by Frankie Beverly and Maze. The song never even hit the first chorus before Poppy would walk downstairs, grumbling the whole way and saying, "Y'all don't know nothing 'bout this." Then he'd start doing some old-school moves he said he did once in a soul train line. I didn't know what the soul train was, or where you could catch it, but it sounded pretty magical.

The music was so loud it shook the walls. Our smiles were so bright they could've lit up the Christmas tree in the town square. And "Before I Let Go" would turn into "September" by Earth, Wind and Fire, and then that would become "We Are Family" by Sister Sledge, and after a while I would be out of breath from trying to keep up with Poppy, and my sides hurting from laughing at my mom's knock-off disco moves.

Mom and I haven't danced together in a long time, though.

Mom said she didn't have as much time to do fun stuff after Poppy died. But really, I think Mom just didn't feel much like dancing anymore. If every day was a celebration in the Before, then every day in the After was a funeral. There's been nothing to shake up the quiet in our house since.

"I can't believe you managed to keep this a secret from me for so long." She shakes her head. "I used to know everything about you, down to the color of your poop when you'd eaten too much dairy."

"Mom!" I shout. She's *so* embarrassing. "Now is really not the time to discuss my irritable baby bowels."

She laughs until a loud knock at our front door makes both of us jump a little.

"Who could it be?" Mom squints to see through the peephole and gasps. She turns to me and whispers, "Ellie, maybe you should go upstairs."

No way am I leaving her down here with someone outside who has her looking like she just found out her favorite TV baker has been using stolen recipes all these years. I pick the chair I'm sitting on just in case I need to use it as a weapon against an intruder and walk on the balls of my feet until I'm behind her. The knocks get even louder.

"Ms. Engle, we'd love to ask you a few questions about your daughter!" a woman's voice shouts from the other side of the door.

My mom rushes over to the big window in our living room

to shut the curtains, but two faces appear before she can pull them closed. The woman from the door has perfectly curled blond hair and she's holding a microphone in her hand. She presses her face against the glass so hard it gets foggy. She looks familiar, but familiar like a teacher you see at the grocery store in their regular clothes—you know who they are, technically, but it's so out of place, it takes a second to figure out what you're seeing.

"Ms. Engle!" The woman spots Mom and smiles brightly. "Where's Frog Girl?"

Just as she starts to wave, a man with a big camera propped on his shoulder turns the lens toward the window and I drop to the floor. Mom pulls the curtains closed and gets on the ground, too, but the woman keeps calling out: "We have security camera footage from her school that proves this wasn't a one-time occurrence! Frog Girl, tell us about the vegetables you revived in the garden—the people need to know!"

Security footage? I didn't even think about the fact that there were cameras in the garden on the day I brought back the radishes. It's gonna be nearly impossible to explain this away to people as just a one-time trick of the light or good editing now. My mind flashes back to using my powers at the mall to heal the plant leaves, and I realize there's probably a lot of evidence out there to expose me. It's only a matter of time before people start digging and come up with enough proof to shatter any hopes I had of keeping this a secret and maybe finding a way to use my powers only to help my mom.

The woman outside's voice gets louder and louder, and finally I realize why she looks and sounds so familiar. I've seen her on our local news pretty much every night of my life. And on billboards all along the highway leading out of town. The too-white teeth, the hairspray-frozen bob, the eyelashes that look more like spider legs under all the makeup. That's Sylvia Joyce Hammett, the Scooper. *She gets the scoop so you're in the loop!*

She has her own theme song and everything.

My face is pressed into the carpet and my hands are over the back of my head. There's a weird stain under my cheek where I'm pretty sure Mom spilled coffee on her way to work recently, but I'm too scared to look up. If I look up, this will be real. If I look up, I can't pretend not to be who I am. *What* I am.

If I look up, my secret will really be out.

"Frog Girl?" My mom's voice is soft, but it sounds like she's laughing. She grabs my fingers and squeezes. "My frog girl."

I open my eyes and she's right there, her face near mine, laid out on the carpet in front of me. I want to cry. I want to scream. I want to shove her car key into her hand so we can escape. But I don't do any of that. I tilt up my chin the best I can and answer in the only way I can think to.

"Ribbit?"

THE NEWS

BREAKING NEWS

Is Indiana's "Frog Girl" proof of Superheroes?

The Pentagon claims "no need to worry" as viral clip suggests that superheroes might, in fact, walk amongst us. "This is no need for alarm", CIA director Mark Joskins said in a press conference this morning. "But we are keeping an eye on the situation".

More on page 4.

LIVE: Plainsboro, IN

Exclusive
TEEN BEHIND "FROG GIRL" VIDEO SPEAKS OUT

2023   KEILOR: "I'M JUST GLAD I COULD EXPOSE THE TRUTH".

ROD DODSON

This is Roddy Doddy, and we know *you* like to party with LA's most listened-to station, 100.4 The Hits! Caller, what's your name?

CALLER 1

Hi, Roddy. Um, this is Greg, longtime listener, first-time caller. I was listening to the story about that little Frog Girl on the show earlier and I wanted to call in to say I think it's a load of crap.

[FART SOUND EFFECT]

ROD DODSON

[Laughs] Well, that's a mighty bold stand to take, Greg. We saw the videos. Heck, the whole *world* has seen the videos by now! The girl touched the frog, and it came to life. She touched those vegetables and they magically grew. Seems like we got a walk-on-water Easter-Sunday resurrection on our hands!

[ANGELIC CHOIR SOUND EFFECT]

CALLER 1

It's a bunch of malarkey, Rod! All this talk of superpowers. Psh! Kids fake this kind of stuff for attention all the time! Give it a week, this will all blow over. She'll get it out of her system, and everything will go back to normal. You'll see.

ROD DODSON

You heard it here first, folks! A bunch of malarkey, or the

real deal, Holyfield? You be the judge! Call in and tell us what you think.

[EXPLOSION SOUND EFFECT]

In other news, America's honorary First Dog, Martian—the prized Pomeranian of international superstar Willa Moon—passed away in his sleep last night. [Voice breaks through tears] The candlelight vigil for the adorable pup is scheduled for tonight at eight p.m. Eastern in front of the Oodles of Noodles on La Cienega, the pup's favorite restaurant.

Rest peacefully, buddy. [Blows nose] We won't be the same without you.

19

Abby sleeps with her cell phone

the way some people sleep with their teddy bears. She cuddles around it with her nose pressed into the glittery hot-pink case as if it's cozy fur instead of hard plastic. The only time it's not in her hand is when she goes to practice.

Seriously. She even takes it to the bathroom.

All day, stories about me have been playing online and on TV. They've even been using the terrible photo of me from sixth-grade picture day when I sneezed half a second before the flash went off, so I have one eye shut and my mouth is screwed up like someone just released an especially nasty fart nearby. There's no way Abby missed all that, or my texts and calls. And even if she had, she couldn't have possibly missed all the commotion in front of our houses—the people just camping out for their chance to get a glimpse at Frog Girl.

There has to be something wrong.

I unlock the latch on my bathroom window and swing one leg out onto the tree branch that brushes against the back of the house. I stop and listen for any noises like Mom waking up or our other neighbor's dog, Goon, barking loud enough to alert the whole neighborhood that I'm breaking out. But Goon is snoring like a chain saw in his doghouse in the Frenches' backyard, and Mom is still asleep in the living room.

Mom hasn't left the living room since last night because, as she said, "If a watched pot never boils, then a watched door should never be broken into." I think her logic might be a little sketchy, but I get it. Everyone wants to see Frog Girl, and she's determined to protect me.

I wrap my arms and legs around the tree trunk and try not to make any noise as the bark scrapes against all my skin. I make a note to self: *Next time you stage a covert breakout attempt to avoid being spotted by the dozens of reporters, men in tinfoil hats who spend all day yelling that you're an abomination, and the Frog Girl fans begging you to sign their autograph books or their babies' foreheads, at least remember to change out of pajamas and into some jeans.*

"Okay, Ellie. That wasn't so bad, was it?" I whisper once I hit the grass. The only answer is the sound of the wind blowing leaves against the side of the house, which I decide to take as a good sign.

I quickly shake out my hands and legs and hit the deck like Black Widow making a daring escape. The small stretch of too-high grass between our house and the Ortegas' may not be as cool as the action scenes she gets to do, but I pat myself on the back for my efforts anyway.

"Oh my goodness, oh my goodness, yuck, yuck." The grass is slimy with dew already, and I can hear the ants tiptoeing across the dirt underneath me. "Abby, I swear to Peter Parker, you owe me so big for this."

I've been texting her nonstop since I left school two days ago, and I haven't gotten a reply yet. At first I was worried that something might have happened to her, like one of the dozens of reporters that showed up on our lawn the first night might have kidnapped her and shaken her down for an inside scoop. But when I saw her walking up the sidewalk with her hair in a high ponytail yesterday, her knee-high cheerleading socks on and her phone pressed to her ear, I realized that maybe there was something else happening. Something I couldn't even wrap my head around.

I somersault as stealthily as I can behind the Ortegas' trash and recycling bins. I test how stable the containers are, and when I decide they're sturdy enough to hold me, I climb on top of them the way Abby taught me to last year when our moms said we couldn't have a sleepover, but we decided to anyway. Trash cans to screened-in porch roof to her bedroom window, just like we practiced. Once I reach her window, it's unlocked, same as always. I shake my head. Abby really should be more careful. There are some real creeps in the world!

"Abby," I hiss, once I land.

I press down on her mattress to shake her awake. She rubs at her nose and smacks her lips together but doesn't wake up. I don't have time for this. I pick up her extra pillow, bring it over my head, and drop it onto her face.

"Wha— What's goin' on?" She sits up and looks around. "Ellie? Oh my god!" Abby hops out of bed and runs over to the window. She pulls it shut and turns to me with her arms crossed. Her voice is quiet, but it's alert. "What are you doing here? Do you know what time it is? I have *school* in the morning!"

Who cares about school? I want to shout. I may never even get to go back to school now that I'm locked up in my bedroom like Rapunzel in her tower. I may never get to do anything normal ever again. Doesn't she get that?

"Why haven't you replied to any of my messages?" I want to sit on her bed, go to sleep, and wake up the night before the first day of school again. When everything between me and Abby was perfect. Before these stupid powers. Before all of it. "I've been trying to talk to you."

Abby bites her lip and looks away. It's her guilty face. The one she makes when she knows she's messed up but doesn't want to admit it.

I know all her expressions better than I know the ones on my own face. Mr. Walker says that sometimes, in super-fancy bakeries, they have what's called a sous baker—the head baker's right hand, their go-to, their number-one supporter. Well, I've always thought of myself as Abby's sous *person*. We've always been there for each other, always been side by side. And somehow, in less than two weeks, everything has changed.

"Well, I've been busy," she mumbles.

"Busy?" I throw my hands up. "That doesn't make any sense. How can you be too busy for me right now? My life is ruined, all thanks to *your* stupid new friend."

"Don't blame Marley for this." She shakes her head, and my eyes start to prickle with tears that I refuse to cry. She's really gonna defend Marley right now? "I told you not to use your powers at school and you did it anyway."

"That was an accident." I blink fast to keep from crying. Why isn't she understanding how hard all this is for me? Why doesn't she get that my whole life is falling apart faster than I can repair it? "Abby, I'm—"

"Famous!" she shouts before remembering that everyone else in the house is asleep. She lowers her voice. "You're famous. Don't you get that? You're all anyone is talking about. 'Frog Girl this, Frog Girl that. Did you see what Frog Girl did? I love Frog

Girl, she's so amazing!'" She makes her voice airy and whiny, and I can't help but wrap my arms around my body like a shield against the sound of it. "Everyone keeps asking me all these questions and I just…I…"

I don't want to know. I wish I'd never come over. I want to undo this whole night.

I can barely breathe.

"You what?"

I think she might not have heard me. But then she glances up and I see it. That look in her eyes. It's the same look from the first time I used my powers to bring back the radishes at school, and the same one from when I told her about the garden I was planting in the backyard to help my mom with the grocery bill. Now, thinking back, the only time I haven't seen that look in Abby's eyes—the only time she's been happy about my powers—was when we used them to prank Bethany.

We've been friends for pretty much our entire lives, and the whole time I've been happy to be a tiny star in Abby's orbit because it meant I got to be around her. I didn't care about the spotlight, I just cared about *her*. I guess I never really considered that maybe the only reason Abby was my best friend wasn't because she was happy to have me around, but because she needed to have someone in her shadow and she just believed that would never change.

"You don't like that there's something that makes me

special now," I answer. "And that all these people are paying attention to me and not you."

My eyes are burning, and my chest is tight. I haven't cried in a long time, at least not in front of another person, but I know that's what's about to happen. My eyes start to spill over, and I can't wipe the tears away fast enough. This doesn't feel real. This whole night—this whole week—seems like some kind of horrible dream sequence in a comic that won't end.

Abby sniffs and wipes at her nose.

"You don't even care about making your mark, and I do," she says, too quiet. Too unlike herself. "It's not fair."

I don't say anything else. I don't think I can. I just walk past her and push the window up as fast as I can. Goon is barking a few houses down, and I can hear one of the reporters scratching a pen across a piece of paper on the sidewalk. But I don't stop. I run across the yard and try to ignore the person who yells, "There she is! It's Frog Girl!" as I push through the back door. The whole yard erupts with noises: cameras clicking, people screaming, babies crying. Once I'm inside, I lean against the door and slide down to the plushy carpet and try to stop crying so hard my shoulders shake and my stomach hurts.

Abby was right.

None of this is fair. It isn't fair at all.

I feel like a deflated soccer ball

when I wake up. I rub at my nose and pull my blankets over my head. Maybe if I pretend I don't exist, everyone will just go away. Maybe if I pretend I don't exist, I can block out everything around me.

But I've never really been the lucky type, so of course that's not what happens. Instead, I hear my mom on the phone in the kitchen, trying to talk quietly enough that I won't be able to hear her. We never got around to testing how far my newfound hearing range stretches, though, so she doesn't know it's no use. She might as well be sitting at the foot of my bed, yelling into a megaphone.

Her voice is as firm as it always is, but she sounds exhausted. I have a feeling this isn't the only time she's had to answer a call like this today. I shut my eyes as if that can help me block her out as well as the chanting on the sidewalk.

"Hey, hey! Ho, ho! Monsters in town have got to go! Hey, hey! Ho, ho! Monsters in town have got to go!"

We thought the Scooper was our biggest problem until the dissection clip hit two million views. It seems like there are more people camped in front of our house than there are residents of Plainsboro. People have set up tents, news vans are lined up and down the street, and a black car with two men in suits inside hasn't moved from the driveway across the street in twenty-four hours. Our front yard is officially a circus full of nosy, unfunny clowns.

Yesterday, one of the tinfoil YouTubers—the people who make videos that either call me a hero or an alien—even tried sneaking into the house by hiding in our garbage can. If Mr. Ortega hadn't noticed and dumped him out all over our driveway, who knows what might have happened?

"I assure you, Mrs. Morelli, this is no reason for me to stop tutoring Lucas," Mom says. "In a few days, this is—"

"It's not right is what it is!" the woman on the other end shouts. "And you, *you're* condoning this behavior like some sort of degenerate! I won't allow it anywhere near my son. Do you hear me?"

The call ends before Mom even gets a chance to respond. Parents don't want their kids to be tutored by the mother of a freak of nature.

"All them people got too much darkness in their hearts," Poppy said once.

A rerun of the old-school *Superman* had just ended, and the eleven o'clock news was showing a bunch of men yelling and throwing bottles and raising these terrible flags in front of a synagogue in New York. It was scary just watching it, so I couldn't imagine what it must have been like for the people inside. It didn't make any sense to me. Why would someone get mad just because people dressed different than they did and prayed in another language?

"Why would they do that?"

I was in second grade, but I was smart for my age—everyone said so. I liked knowing stuff. My teachers always said that knowledge was power, after all, and I wanted to be powerful. I wanted to stop my parents from yelling at each other. Stop Poppy from being sad about missing Gramma Candy. That was back before I learned that knowing by itself doesn't always fix what's broken. That the people who can save everyone and everything are the ones in tights and capes, and they aren't ever gonna show up, so it's better to leave the heroes on the page.

I pointed at the screen. "Those people didn't even do anything!"

Poppy reached for the remote and muted the TV. I felt better when I couldn't hear those men shouting anymore.

"You know why so many superheroes wear masks?" Poppy asked. When I shook my head, he scratched his beard for a second. "It's 'cause people like being saved, so long as they never have to know who's doing the saving. When a person has a name and a face, they become human. And with some people, if they realize another human is something they'll never be, can do something they just weren't built to do, then sometimes they get real hateful."

I didn't get it right away, and I didn't want to ask. I wanted to go back to watching Clark Kent get nervous about being around Lois Lane. That was easy. But what Poppy was trying to teach me wasn't. It was one of the hardest lessons I ever learned.

That there are a lot of people who hate what they can't understand—who love power, but only if they can control it. And nobody knows how to control a girl who can do the unthinkable, not even me.

When I get downstairs, my mom has her head in her hands. She's leaning against the counter, and there are envelopes spread out in front of her. Too many of them have a red stamp on the front that says FINAL NOTICE.

I know she wants me to have the best life I can. But she never gets enough sleep, and the lines around her mouth look like she frowns more than she smiles. She's given up so much, and now she's lost jobs because of me. I feel so guilty it makes my mouth taste like I swallowed a fistful of pennies.

And suddenly the thought of being in the house for another second feels like too much to handle. There aren't many places I can go in town without being spotted by a journalist immediately, or worse, reported to my mom. But there's one place that's always been safe, always made me feel protected from everything else in the world.

So, before Mom looks up and spots me, I run back upstairs to my room. I grab the crate full of my favorite comic books, a flashlight, and a pair of big noise-canceling headphones that have been collecting dust under my bed and drag them both into my mom's closet. I shut the door behind me, crawl to the back where the bag of my dad's leftover clothes sits, and lean against the wall.

It's been a long time since I did this. Been a long time since I felt like disappearing and didn't know how else to do it. But sliding on the headphones and clicking on the flashlight to illuminate the crate of comic books is just like riding a bike. It takes me back to my safe space. Shuts out the world and the noise and makes it easier to imagine that things are as simple as they used to be.

When Mom was still only working at the bakery and Dad kissed her the minute he came in the door. When Abby didn't resent me for powers I couldn't control. When Poppy was still alive and I always had someone around who wanted to believe in remarkable things, even while living in the most unremarkable place on earth.

I run my hands over the row of R comics. *Radioactive Man. Raggedy Ann and Andy. Ragnarok.* I let myself get lost in it, just the feeling of the plastic sleeves under my fingers and the simple rhythm of reciting the titles. I pluck one out at random, take it out of its sleeve, and flip it open to the first page. When I do, a small photo flutters out and lands in my lap.

It's a picture of me and Poppy dressed up as Shuri and T'Challa for HeroCon, this big convention where people who love comic books can go and get exclusive issues and meet other fans and even see some of the actors from the big superhero movies. I run my fingers over the picture of the two of us posing back-to-back in front of the convention center. I couldn't have been any older than first grade. Poppy looked so serious, but I couldn't stop laughing. He carried me on his shoulders for half the day, and the other half we spent finding rare issues of comics and getting our books signed by their authors and illustrators. It was one of the best memories I have of those simple days.

"You would think having powers was cool, I bet. You would tell me to embrace them," I say to his picture. "You'd probably say: 'Well, Ellie-girl, any kind of hero you want to be is the right kind. So, you better get to figuring out what that looks like.'"

I shake my head. Poppy always wanted me to do and be whatever made me feel the most myself. But that's just the thing—for the longest time, I was whatever Abby wasn't. If she was loud, I was quiet. If she was bold, I was boring. If she wanted to make her mark, I tried to ensure that I never left a trace of myself anywhere. Now I'm stuck with these powers, and just when I was starting to think they could be cool, they managed to blow up my whole life. I don't know what I want to do anymore, but I know that it doesn't matter how hard I hope, there's no going back to the way things were before.

I slide the photo of me and Poppy back between the pages and slip the book back into its plastic sleeve.

"Okay. So maybe this is bad, but it probably won't get any worse, right?" I try to reassure myself. "Maybe I just stop using my powers completely until everything blows over."

I nod, my mind made up. No more powers for now for any reason. Not to spy or to make food or to prank bullies. Nothing. I'll keep a low profile, and maybe all of this will blow over. And then me and Mom can figure out what to do about my whole supernatural situation. I slide the headphones off my ears, and immediately the sound of a commotion downstairs hits me full force. There are too-fast voices, and fingernails clicking across phone screens, and my mom's worried questions rising up in the middle of everything.

I drop the crate of comic books and run downstairs. I have no idea what's going on, but something tells me that whatever it is, I'm the only person who can fix it.

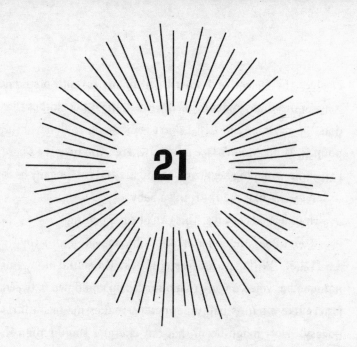

The world's most famous celebrity is drinking from a chipped Avengers mug

that I painted in third-grade art class when I run into the kitchen. I skid to a stop on the hardwood floor and practically pass out at the sight.

"Mom, what is Willa Moon doing at our kitchen table?"

The second I say her name, Willa stands and extends her hands in my direction. I'm freaking out. I'm really freaking out. Before this I'd seen her face in movies and on TV, on billboards, in stores, on posters in Abby's room, and on an old

DeeDee the Detective T-shirt I got for my seventh birthday that's somewhere under my bed with all the other clothes that don't fit anymore but that I don't want Mom to donate. The point is, Willa Moon's face is everywhere. And now she's here in person, wrapping her arms around me and rubbing my back in soft circles like she's burping a baby.

Thunderbolts of Jove. This can't be happening.

Mom hisses under her breath, "She says she *knows you*."

"Elliot," Willa says as she steps back. The sound of my full name in her voice, a voice that bounces up and down between letters like a tennis ball on concrete, makes me feel a little queasy. "How magnificent that our energies should align in this way."

"Um..." What energies? How are they *aligned*, and how do I get them to, I don't know, unalign again? "Thank you? I think?"

Willa looks to her right. For the first time since I came downstairs, I pay attention to something other than how unreal it is to be near someone who has eaten brunch on Beyoncé's private island. Next to her is a serious-looking Black woman in a gray suit and extra-high red heels. She has on the kind of red lipstick that makes her look intimidating and powerful. Like if she punched you in the nose, your head might actually separate from your body. Yikes.

And behind her is a man clicking around on his phone. He's doesn't seem to be paying any attention to the rest of us, but something about how fast his fingers are moving on his screen tells me he means business. Both of them seem so different from Willa, it's hard to comprehend that they showed up here together.

Willa looks like if you touched her, your hand would go straight through. It's different when she's in movies because her hair is always a darker color: fire-engine red, jet black, a soft brown. But in real life, her long, straight hair is so blond it's almost white. Her skin is so pale it's almost see-through. Her eyes are so green... Well, her eyes are pretty normal, actually. Regular old green-ish brown. Which makes me feel a little better about the whole thing.

She nods and waves her hand in the air. Just like that, the man with the phone bends down to grab a big pink purse off the floor and he hands it to her. A furry little head pops out of the top, and a pink tongue flops out of his mouth.

"Monkey, say hello," Willa says.

Oh my goodness, this is *Monkey* in my kitchen! The spokesdog for every company from Pizza Hut to Gucci barks once.

Willa smiles down at him and then at me. How are her teeth so straight?

"Elliot, I come to you humbly. As a mother in need."

I turn to face my mom, and she looks just as confused as I feel. Her arms are crossed over her chest and her forehead has more wrinkles than ever. For the first time ever, she looks like she's waiting for me to tell her how to handle this. Like

I'm supposed to have a better idea about why these people are here than she does.

"Look, kid." The man slides his iPhone into his pocket and puffs out his chest. Like Willa, his accent isn't one from around here. His voice is so big it fills up the whole room. "You ever heard of Martian?"

Willa lets out a loud sob at the name of her precious dog and falls into the chair she was sitting in when I showed up. Monkey and Martian were twin Pomeranians, and Willa is never caught out in public without them. They're almost as famous as she is. Honestly, if they could learn to sing, Willa would be out of a job in a heartbeat.

But Martian passed away yesterday, and pretty much the whole country feels about it like Willa does. As if Martian had belonged to all of us. But I don't know what that has to do with me.

The man continues. "We know you got the . . . the—what're we calling it? The powers or whatever? Willa needs you to bring Martian back to life."

"No. Absolutely not." It's the first thing Mom has said since Willa started speaking. She lowers her voice and turns to Willa, who's still dabbing at her teary eyes. "No offense. I'm very sorry for your loss. Martian was a lovely performer. We were big fans of *This Dog Hates Smog.*"

His show about the effects of pollution on the pet population was amazing. Martian was a great journalist.

My mom turns back to the man in the suit. "My child won't be participating in the Willa Moon media circus."

The thing about Willa Moon is that she isn't just famous—she's *fame*. She pretty much sets the standard for what it means to be popular in the biggest way possible. She has movies and music, a clothing line and a makeup deal, a vegan spaghetti company, and a stainless-steel cookware collection at Bed, Bath & Beyond. But the thing that makes her impossible to escape—the thing that made her the most famous person in the world—is her reality show: *The Moon and More*. Every episode, she does something more spectacular, more outrageous than the episode before.

Like last season, me and Abby had a viewing party by making a fort in her living room and popping caramel kettle corn to watch the momentous occasion that was Willa (and Monkey and Martian) literally going to space. And okay, technically, she didn't make it to space, because the rocket was still being beta tested and could legally only break through like two layers of the earth's atmosphere, but still! She was the first self-proclaimed "Virgo moon ethereal spirit being" to make it that far, so obviously it was a big deal. According to the news, it was the most viewed episode of a semi-scripted Kids Choice Award–nominated cable-network reality television show *ever*.

You don't say no when Willa Moon shows up. Especially when—

"Look, we'll pay you a million dollars," the man says.

Oh. Um. *What?*

"But you gotta do it on the show. The people want to see it, and we need a season finale that'll blow last season's 'Brunch with Beyoncé' episode out of the water...so."

"I don't get it." I shake my head. A million dollars? That's more money than my mom makes in ten years—more than she'll make in her entire life! "You don't even know if I really can do it."

Willa practically glides back in front of me and cups my cheeks in her hands and...Oh my goodness, she smells like flowers and glitter. I didn't even know glitter *had* a smell! My mouth kind of flops open like a fish as she smiles down at me.

"I believe in the ineffable." She nods. "Do *you* believe in the unbelievable, Elliot Engle?"

I bob my head slowly. I don't think I can form words right now. I'm pretty sure my brain has officially turned the OPEN FOR BUSINESS sign to CLOSED FOR GOOD and is on vacation in the Bahamas. I can't wrap my head around what she's saying or what the suit guy is offering. All I can imagine are those stacks of unpaid bills Mom thinks I don't know about, and the way she falls asleep in the middle of a sentence sometimes because she's so exhausted.

This could be the answer I've been searching for. This could be our ticket out.

But if I do this, if I go on camera on the most popular reality show in the world, then there will be no chance of returning to even the slightest sense of normal. No hiding. If I do this, that's it. I'll be Frog Girl forever.

"Then we shall proceed in faith." Willa leans forward and presses her forehead to mine. "Angelique will assist you." She turns to my mom, and hands her a—*pineapple*? Where did she even get that? "Àṣẹ."

And with that, Willa sweeps out with Monkey, leaving Angelique behind to shove a stack of papers into my mom's hand—the one that isn't holding the pineapple. They talk in low, fast tones, but I can't even keep up. Because I'm still looking at the door that the biggest celebrity in the world disappeared through, wondering what the heck just happened.

My superpower used to be invisibility

before all of this. I could stand in a room with a hundred people and almost disappear. And while I was there, fading into the background, Abby would be in the center doing backflips in a sequined leotard or something. I was good with things being that way. The girl in the background doesn't owe anyone anything—doesn't have to have answers for questions that feel impossible to understand. There's only the world I build for myself and the worlds I get lost in in my comic books.

Some people are meant to be in the spotlight. And some people, people like me, are meant to watch from the wings. Or, at least that's what I always thought.

When Willa's lawyer leaves, and Mom is at the kitchen table with her face in the stack of paperwork Willa left behind, I disappear into my bedroom. It looks the same as always—walls plastered with vintage Justice League posters Poppy would get me for my birthday every year, piles of clothes on the floor that I'm always too lazy to put in the hamper in the closet, a bookshelf with stacks on stacks of back issues and graphic novels. It feels weird to stand in it and know that even though everything in it is the way it's always been, I couldn't be more different.

I flop down on the floor next to Burt the Betta Fish's bowl. He glug-glugs at the glass, and I press my finger against it gently. You can't pet fish, obviously, so this is as close as I can get. I let myself focus on the soft swish-swish of his tail in the water for so long my eyes get a little dry and I start to doze off. It makes me feel like a kindergartener again. Like, if I just curl up and take a nap, when I wake up, my mom will hand me a juice box and a snack, and my biggest problem will be whether a new episode of *Doc McStuffins* is on soon or not.

But then someone starts knocking on the door, and no juice box can make me forget that nothing is the way it was in kindergarten. I hear Bree's voice before my mom calls up the stairs to tell me she's here.

"Ellie?"

"Down here." I groan and roll over onto my back.

Bree comes around the side of the bed and frowns when she sees me on the floor, but she doesn't ask any questions. She just sits down with her back against the wall and extends her legs. If anyone knows how to sit in the quiet, it's Breonna Boyd, but after a few minutes, I can't help but ask what she's doing here. No one has come to see me except reporters and protesters and one very odd world-famous celebrity since, well, everything.

"Mrs. Harlow said you hadn't picked up your homework." She pulls her backpack into her lap and unzips the top. "I didn't want you to fall behind just because..."

"Because I'm a walking freak show?"

I sit up and tuck my knees up to my chest. I haven't even thought about homework. How could I? If there's a necromancer who just waltzes back into seventh grade all willy-nilly after having the weirdest dissection resurrection in history streamed live and in color for half the world to see, I certainly haven't read their comic yet.

"You shouldn't say that." Bree's voice is serious. "Just because you're different doesn't make you a freak."

I know I'm pouting like a big baby, but I can't help myself. I wish I could just scream and kick my legs in the air until the walls come down.

"Why not?" I ask. "That's what everyone is saying. That I'm an *abomination*."

I can hear people chanting it outside our house all day, and even when they stop, it sometimes plays on a loop in my head. Mom stopped turning on the TV yesterday because people on some news channel were getting so mean with what they were saying, but not before I heard it. They don't just think I shouldn't have these powers—they think I shouldn't even exist.

I try to be as grown-up as I can. I try to help my mom by not complaining. But I'm not a grown-up. I'm a kid. How can people say a kid shouldn't exist?

People think they want to believe in superheroes. That's why the Avengers movies make a zillion dollars apiece and why they've had, like, seven hundred different versions of Superman over the past fifty years. Because losing yourself in the fantasy of the all-good and all-powerful is reassuring. But they don't want superheroes. Not in real life. They want cardboard cut-outs. And I'm too human for them.

"Do you really think that?" Bree asks. She nervously plucks at the hem of her T-shirt. "That you're what they say you are?"

"I mean, no." I shrug. "I have powers, yeah, but I'm not some kind of monster."

I rub at my eyes and try to keep from getting all emotional. I gulp down a big breath and clear my throat before I do something embarrassing like cry in front of Bree. She probably never cries. She's so together all the time.

"They can't make you into something you're not," she says after a beat of silence. The corners of her lips flick up for a split second. Her voice gets higher and more excited the more she explains. "What you can do is so cool—so useful. You could change the world with the tips of your fingers. Not every person with powers is that lucky. I mean, I wish I—"

She stops herself and shrugs, almost like she forgot for a second that she doesn't usually let herself get worked up about much of anything.

"Anyways, that's the trade-off for heroes, right?" she says, soft and quiet like usual. She pushes her glasses up with one finger. "With great power comes great responsibility and all that."

I shake my head, even though she's right. Of course, being a superhero is about power and responsibility—that's like the first lesson of any origin story. But that's the thing: I'm not a hero. I'm just a kid with powers that I don't understand and didn't want, and now the whole world knows my name. I'm not supposed to save the world. Without Willa's show, I can't even save my mom. I can't even save *me*.

My head starts spinning with all the things that could go wrong. What if Martian's already been dead for too long to revive him? What if my powers choose now to completely poop out on me? What if doing something like this, making my mark in front of the entire world, is me flushing any hopes at ever being friends with Abby again down the toilet?

"Yeah, but…" I try to find the words. I look around my room until my eyes stop on a poster of a Wonder Woman special issue hanging over my dresser. "Look at Wonder Woman. She was born to be a hero, right? To be *great*." I stretch out my legs until they're parallel with Bree's. "Not everybody gets their whole life to train to do something amazing in front of the entire world. Some of us just get … stuck."

She makes a quiet *hmm* sound and nods. "I read this thing once—"

"Of course you did," I say, and she nudges her sock-covered toe against my ribs with an eye roll.

"About reluctant heroes. About why every 'chosen one' story pretty much starts the same. Star Wars. The Hunger Games. Frog Girl."

I groan and bury my face in my hands, but Bree keeps talking.

"It's because people want to believe that we're all capable of doing something great. That each of us, even the wallflowers, can change the world."

Reluctant hero. I bounce the words around in my brain a couple of times and try it on for size. She's definitely right about the reluctant part. I don't think there's ever been anyone less interested in having earth-shattering powers than me. But that doesn't change the fact that I have them. That I can do something important with them, even if I have to do it in front of the entire world.

"You're wrong about me, you know."

"How?" I wipe my nose on the hem of my shirt. I've gotta be the messiest superhero in the world, saying all sorts of things on accident and snotting all over a perfectly good T-shirt. "What did I say?"

Bree links her fingers together in her lap and twists her thumbs around each other nervously.

"I cry sometimes." She looks at me. "I'm not as together as I look. You know what they say about judging a book by its cover."

"That sometimes the cover is the best part of the story?" I smirk.

Bree sticks her tongue out at me before letting out a soft laugh. "For someone who can do something as serious as control life and death, you sure do make a lot of jokes."

"What can I say?" I shrug. "Necromancers are people, too. We gotta get our comedy someplace."

I don't know how Bree manages to pull me out of my pity party so fast, but she's done it twice. Once at the mall, and now. She's right about me sometimes judging a book by its cover. I never thought she would be the best person I knew to talk to when I'm feeling bummed out, but she is. I want to thank her for being here and just sitting with me like I'm a normal person, but I don't know how. So I try to keep making things as normal as possible.

"So, what kind of homework are we dealing with?" I ask.

Bree walks me through a project that we have coming up in Language Arts, and I'm actually kind of excited about it. We have to get in groups of three to come up with a presentation about *The Giver*, our summer reading. I liked the book a lot, even though I think having homework over the summer should be against the law. By the time she's done explaining, I realize

I've smiled more in twenty minutes than I have in all the days I've been trapped in my dungeon bedroom.

"When all this dies down, are you gonna come back to school?" she asks.

I don't know. I can barely even think about what's gonna happen tomorrow without wanting to puke a little bit. I definitely can't wrap my brain around what it'll be like going back to school. But I know I can't hide out here forever. If for no other reason than unfortunately my mom isn't willing to go to jail for harboring a fugitive of the truant variety. For real, I already asked.

"Maybe. I guess."

"Well, you should," she says seriously, and then her lips quirk up a little. "I can't deal with Marley Keilor without you."

She starts packing her stuff up to leave, but I don't want her to go. I kind of need her to stay for a little while longer so I don't completely lose my marbles worrying about this Willa Moon thing. I barely even think about it before I blurt out: "Wait! You wanna stay for a while?"

She looks up, all surprised, like I'm speaking some kind of foreign language.

"Maybe watch a movie?" I add.

It takes her a second, but she finally nods.

"I just have to call my mom and see if it's okay, but, um, I'd like that. To stay."

I'm so excited, I almost trip over my feet running to get my mom's laptop. While Bree is calling home—I try not to eavesdrop, but I can't help but do an internal cheer when I hear her mom say "That's fine, but no later than eight"—I boot up the most recent Wonder Woman adaptation.

Wonder Woman 1984 isn't my favorite superhero movie, but it's pretty good. If nothing else, the goofy clothes from the eighties are always fun to laugh at. By the time we get settled on a stack of pillows on the floor and the first few minutes of the movie have passed, even Bree can't keep in her giggles. One of the characters comes on-screen with a hairdo that probably used up so much hairspray it ruined the ozone. When I say as much, Bree laughs so hard she snorts. I take that as a win.

The whole movie is about responsibility and sacrifice, two things that would probably be at the top of any superhero school curriculum. There's a stone that grants wishes, but every wish comes with a price. When it falls into the hands of a man who wants all the money and power in the world, Wonder Woman has to stop him before he pretty much destroys the planet. But even Wonder Woman can't help but get a wish granted, and she ends up bringing her boyfriend back to life.

"He's cute for an old man," Bree says, pointing at Steve Trevor.

"Maybe." I shrug. "Hippolyta is super old, but I think she's cuter."

I want to take back the words as soon as they're out of my

mouth. Most girls don't admit that they think other girls are cute, at least not in the way boys are. But Bree doesn't seem grossed out or scared or anything. She just nods.

"Hmm," she hums. "And she could beat up Steve Trevor with just her pinkie." I feel a warm glow in my chest that I think might be relief. "That makes her infinitely cuter."

We watch the rest of the movie mostly without adding any comments. Eventually, Wonder Woman starts to lose some of her strength to keep Steve Trevor alive as the trade-off for having her wish granted. I think about what Poppy would say about giving something up to get something else.

"Everything is give and take, girl. That's just how it is. Gotta keep the scales of the universe balanced, otherwise everything falls outta whack," he said once after we read one of the *Justice League* issues where the wish-granting stone showed up. "That's just the cost of admission."

Poppy was a cranky old man, but he made some good points.

"See?" Bree says as the movie ends. She shakes her head like a disappointed old lady, and when she pushes her glasses up the bridge of her nose, it just drives home the point. "Like my mom always says, men are nothing but trouble."

"Amen, sister."

I hold my hand up in a high five, and we both laugh until I can barely remember what I was scared of.

23

I have the biggest wedgie of my life

but there are way too many cameras around for me to feel comfortable plucking my underwear. This is one thing they don't tell you about reality TV: Not being able to pick at your butt without a million people making you into a meme is easily the number-one worst part. Except the part where you're asked to do a resurrection live on camera for enough money to change your life forever and confirm once and for all that you're able to defy the laws of nature, thus opening yourself up to a lifetime of questions and publicity and no privacy and absolute isolation from any and every person you've ever loved.

That little, itty, bitty, tiny part.

"Belly, isn't this a bit . . . much?"

My mom looks around the room and shuts her eyes against the too-bright lights. It only took twenty-four hours after her visit for Willa's crew to show up in town with all of their cameras and supplies. The lights are hanging from the ceiling, propped up on tall, skeleton-like stands, and stuck to the walls. It's brighter in here than it is outside.

Willa's team sent us a fancy black car this morning that took us to a fake house a town over. Well, the house is real, I guess, it's just not the house we actually live in. It's too perfect. There's a too-green lawn in the front, and a white picket fence around the yard. Inside, it looks a lot like the kind of house where they film TV shows with two kids, a goofy dad, a really smart, overworked mom, and a laugh track. The whole place smells like fresh paint.

"This place is better for aesthetics, kid. Don't worry too much about it," the man who's always on the phone said when we showed up an hour ago.

His name, turns out, is Dominick, and he's Willa's manager. But from the amount of talking and texting he does, it sounds like he's her personal assistant, scheduler, agent, and spiritual guide all in one. He's a little too intense for me, so I've been avoiding him by hiding out in one of the bedrooms upstairs that they turned into a makeup studio and dressing room. Apparently, not only was our house not good enough for TV, but neither were my clothes.

"Sweetheart, no. That is *not* gonna play well on camera."

An older white woman with long, frizzy salt-and-pepper hair shook her head at me when I walked in wearing a white T-shirt with black stripes—the only shirt I own that doesn't have some sort of character or logo or saying on it—and black jeans. She immediately shoved into my hands a denim dress with buttons all the way up the front and a tie at the waist and shooed me back behind a curtain. When I came out, she made me trade my Converse for a pair of black booties with fringe on the side and a little heel. The whole look made me feel like a phony, but I just bit my tongue.

"It's good." I nod and try not to sound like I'm convincing myself. I tug at the too-snug tie around my middle and pretend like this is fine. Everything is great. "Don't wanna look bad on TV, right?"

I smile, but it's pretty pathetic. The truth is, I'm terrified. Nothing about this screams *Great idea, Ellie!* except the stack of papers Mom and me spent two hours going through last night, after Bree left, with the big, bolded ONE MILLION USD printed across a couple of the pages. Even Mom couldn't shake how much good all that money would do for us.

I didn't miss the long breath Mom let out when I signed my name across the bottom in some squiggly lines that I hoped passed as cursive. So maybe I wasn't the kind of superhero who could save the world, but I might be able to save the two of us.

I want to send a text to Abby asking if she thinks this is

the right thing to do. I want to check in with her like I always have. But then I remember that Abby doesn't want to talk to me anymore, and that she hates everything my powers represent. Even thinking about Abby makes my stomach hurt. I try to settle myself down before I do the worst thing imaginable and barf all over Willa Moon's designer platform sandals on national TV. I'd never recover from that one.

"All right, people, let's get this show on the road!" The director claps his hands together from the living room. He kind of reminds me of the movie version of Tony Stark: short, loud, and convinced he's the boss even though pretty much everyone in the room has a more important job than him.

And then, in a voice too quiet for anyone but me to hear, he adds, "I'd like to get back to LA before I get some airborne disease from this hick town."

Okay, I take back what I said about him being like Tony Stark. He doesn't even deserve that much. He's one of the rats that eat the trash behind Stark Industries.

"Somebody get the kid!" he yells so loud I bring my shoulders up to my ears.

When I walk to the center of the room, it's the first time since I arrived that everyone behind the scenes actually sees me. I know most of their names from overhearing bits and pieces of conversations—Jimmy and Kevin are on lights, Tia and John and Dion are on sound, June and Carlos are working the cameras, and then Sean and Marta and Jack and Danny and Ben are doing jobs I don't understand, but they're wearing headsets, so they must be important. But that's a one-way street.

I know things I'm not supposed to know because my powers make it impossible not to. But for everyone else, this is their first time seeing me outside of a video or hearing my voice other than the shout I let out when Marley started to blurt out my secret. Some people try to focus on the job they're doing, but the whole room gets quiet when I step into the light. People stand straighter, their heartbeats speed up, and breaths get sharper.

For the first time in my life, people aren't just noticing me in passing, they're reacting. And beyond that, they're *afraid*.

"Could we die if she touches us?" Kevin whispers.

"I don't know, but I'm not going anywhere near her," Jimmy mumbles back.

My hands start to sweat, and my head begins to pound. I'm not just a freak of nature to them. I'm a monster.

And the whole world is about to know.

24

A dog is biting at my ankle

and the sight of him makes me smile, even though I kind of feel like passing out again because of what I'm about to do. I crouch down to pet behind his fluffy little ears. Ears that are so adorable, I heard once that they're insured for, like, a billion dollars. His tongue lolls out of his mouth, and he rolls over on his back so I'll scratch his belly. It's so normal, I almost forget where I am until Willa's flowy voice starts speaking.

"Our spirits called to each other, Elliot. Today, we answer."

"You can, um, call me Ellie," I say.

I'm about to bring her dog back to life in front of millions of people—I feel like now is a good time to get personal.

"Ellie," Willa says, her voice all soft and singsongy.

This whole thing is weird, but honestly, I think Willa may be the weirdest part of all. I don't even understand half of the things she says. She dabs at her eyes with a white tissue. I know she's saying the words—like, I can see her mouth moving and everything—but she sounds sort of weird. Like she's reading from a script. If there's a script for how we're supposed to handle something this big, I definitely didn't get one.

"You were meant to come into our lives at this very moment."

She pushes open the top of the shiny white coffin on the table in front of us. Inside, tucked between hot-pink silk, is Martian. I can't help but gasp and cover my mouth when I see him.

It's creepy, I can't lie. With Burt the Betta Fish and the radishes and the frog in class, everything happened so fast that there was no time to really think about what I was doing. I just sort of did it. Whether it was on accident or on purpose, I've never *tried* to bring a dead thing back to life when people expected it of me (the failed resurrection of Abby's pet guinea pig doesn't count, obviously). When I look down at Martian in his tiny dog coffin, he looks like he's just taking a nap. Like, if I didn't know any better, things could be normal.

Or, I don't know, maybe this *is* normal. The circle of life and all that. He's only been dead for about three days, and I brought back the frog in science under way worse conditions. So I don't think the question is if I *can* do this—I think the question might be *should* I do this? Not just because of my privacy, or because I'd like to go through the rest of my life pretending to be totally normal, but because I don't know if it should be up to me to decide who—or what—lives or dies. It's the kind of pressure that should be saved for people with lots of training and experience and, I don't know, a million years of medical school. Not a twelve-year-old girl who practically fell out of bed and into a superpower less than two weeks ago.

Ms. Winston would probably say this is about ethics, but when I look up, and everyone in the room is staring at me, I know it's not really about what's right or wrong. That would be way easier. It's about the fact that a world-famous celebrity asked me to do something, and it wasn't the kind of thing you say no to. It's about the fact that I have a power that can do something big enough to make sure my mom doesn't have to worry about money for a long, long time. It's about the fact that I don't know what I'm supposed to do, and I'm really scared, and I just want to be the kind of hero Poppy would be proud of.

On the other side of the table, Willa's face is bright and hopeful, even though she hasn't stopped crying since the cameras started rolling. She nods at me and tilts her head at Martian. The motion is super subtle, so I'm pretty sure she doesn't want the camera to pick up on it. Does she know what

I'm thinking? Can she see in my face that I don't want to do this? That I don't know what I'm doing?

I gulp.

The director sent my mom into the other room so she could watch on a small screen while staying out of the way, but I want her to be by my side. I'm feeling all shaky and nervous, and it's like kindergarten all over again. I just want my mommy.

"Willa, I..." I start, but then I look over her shoulder, and Dominick is in the corner shaking his head. He doesn't have a phone in his hand anymore. This time, he's waving a big stack of dollar bills like he knows exactly what I'm thinking. "I'm, uh, glad our energies aligned?"

Willa puts her hands together like she's praying and bows in my direction.

Okay. I can do this. It's easy. All I have to do is touch him, and he'll come back to life. Touch him, and we'll get a million dollars. And, who knows? Maybe Abby will actually *want* to talk to me when she sees me on TV with her idol, Willa Moon. She'll have to ask me what it was like to talk to her, to hug her, to pet Monkey on his perfect little head, won't she?

And it's that thought more than anything that helps me swallow all my nerves. The thought that maybe this could also be a ticket to getting Abby to be my friend again.

The whole room feels like it leans forward with me as I hold my hands out over Martian. The lights get hotter, the long microphone over my head gets lower, the camera people inch closer. I take a breath. I close my eyes. I press both hands to Martian's fur.

"Yip!"

Martian pops up and licks my hand, and I let out a huge breath. I hoped I could do it, but I thought that maybe—

"Oh my god!" Willa shouts, and covers her mouth with both hands.

"What's going on?" Dominick rushes out of the corner. "What'd you do?"

I look around the room, confused. Martian is happy and healthy. His paws are up on the side of his no-longer-coffin and he's barking like he's never been more alive. And then I look down.

"My baby!" Willa drops down to the ground. Monkey is on his side, legs stiff and eyes closed. "You killed my baby!"

I drop to the wood floor and ignore the way my knees thud against the ground. Oh no. Oh no. Oh no, no, no, no, no. This doesn't make any sense! Nothing like this was supposed to happen!

"I don't understand." I shake my head. I press my hands to Monkey's fur, just like I'd done Martian's, but Monkey doesn't move. I press my ear to his little chest, hoping that I'll be able to hear something, anything, that tells me he's still in there. But there's nothing.

I don't know how. I don't know why. But I somehow just managed to pull off the most dysfunctional reanimation in history for the most famous person in the world.

"This isn't— I didn't—"

I stop. Oh my goodness. This is Wonder Woman and Steve Trevor. This is the sacrifice. This is what it means to gain something you've always wanted but to lose something you never thought to give up. This is the real-life cost of using your powers recklessly or for your own gain. My brain flashes back to Ms. Winston finding dead tomato plants in the garden the morning after I resurrected the radishes. I can hear Poppy's voice on a loop in my brain: *Everything is give and take.*

Everything. Beginning with life and death.

I shake my head like if I say no enough times it can undo everything I've done, but I know that's impossible. I've read enough comic books to know when something is irreversible.

"Dominick." Willa's face changes from its usual soft, angelic expression to something a little more Hulk-like. And I don't mean Bruce Banner, either. I mean full-on, hundred-foot-tall, green, grunting giant.

She points at me and literally growls. "Cut the cameras."

Uh-oh.

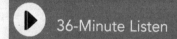

LORI MACY, HOST: This is *Deep Waters*, the International Public Radio podcast where we interview artists, thinkers, and scientists about the stories that move them. I'm your host, Lori Macy.

Everyone wants to believe that there are powers beyond us, something greater than what we know, what we see, what we can touch. For generations, we've bought into narratives that simultaneously confound the mind and spark our imaginations. The aliens at Area 51. The Loch Ness monster traversing the waters of the Scottish Highlands. And recently, the infamous, and now notorious, Frog Girl.

[SOUNDBITE OF PAPARAZZI QUESTIONING WILLA MOON AT LAX]

WILLA MOON: I'm directing all further questions to my medical spokesperson, Dr. Bill. Please respect my family's privacy during these unprecedented times.

MACY: On the pod today, we welcome Dr. Bill McCaw, host of the show *That's Not My Baby with Dr. Bill.** Dr. Bill, thank you for joining us.

MCCAW: It's a pleasure to be here, lil' lady.

MACY: Well, that's a bit patronizing, but it's great to have you. You've been quite outspoken about the Frog Girl story recently, and the whole world is interested in what went wrong there. Is this a case of mass delusion?

MCCAW: This is a common case of what we in the medical field like to call "a mule looking at a grass sack."

MACY: Oh, I've never heard of—

MCCAW: Well, it's under-researched, but let me assure you it's absolutely real and there's no need to look it up to fact-check me. [LAUGHS NERVOUSLY.] This young lady believed she had the ability to perform some sort of necromancy— probably as a result of lack of love in the home, fatherlessness . . . any number of issues, really—and it manifested itself in a fallacy she managed to get the entire world to believe. It's quite common in girls of her ilk, though we rarely see it on this scale.

This young woman is a fraud, pure and simple. And unfortunately, when she saw a viable target for her validation—Ms. Moon, in her grief—she attempted to take advantage. And when she failed, obviously, to complete the resurrection she promised she could do, Ms. Moon was rightfully devastated. It's a case of exploitation, attention-seeking, and just plain preteen lying. And I hope this young woman learned her lesson: You can't pee down America's leg and tell us it's rainin'.

*We're legally required to state that Dr. Bill has had his license to practice psychiatric medicine revoked in California, Texas, and the Federated States of Micronesia. Listener discretion is advised.

SCOOP MAG

Issue n. 144/ September 2023

FRAUD

"FROG GIRL"
FAKE:
THE SHOCKER OF
THE DECADE

Willa Moon
speaks out an
imposter
25

Exclusive
interview with
Monkey
43

How to strain
your pasta

56

THE RIBBIT:
The Official
Frog Girl fan site

My Take on the situation

Hi Frog Fans, it's Emmy here, moderator of The Ribbit, finally ready to speak out on the situation with Willa Moon and our queen; Frog Girl. The way I see it, Frog Girl refused to do Willa's stupid show, and Willa decided to save face by claiming that Frog Girl wouldn't help her out, and because she always gets her way, she started a smear campaign to make it seem like Frog Girl was faking her powers for attention.

All of this is just the bitter blowback of a spoiled, washed up, child star. Here at The Ribbit, we stand by our girl, and will continue to be the go-to site for all future Frog Girl updates.

And as always, hop on!

TO SUPPORT FROG GIRL, DONATE TO THE FROG GIRL DEFENSE FUND <u>HERE</u>

25

Mr. Walker is not a good babysitter

but he is crazy good at baking blueberry pancake cupcakes, so when Mom tells me I have to stay with him at the bakery all day while she goes to look for a new part-time tutoring job, it's not such a bad thing. Besides, being inside Patty's Cakes is almost like being inside a fairy tale. Everything is pumped full of enough sugar to fuel the cars in the Indy 500, and frosted and decorated so adorably that it could have been straight out of a picture book. I couldn't ask for anything better, really.

It helps that as long as I'm at the bakery, that means I'm not at school. Which I really, really am not ready for.

"Mr. Walker!" I call the minute I step into the bakery. It takes him a second, but eventually he walks out of the kitchen.

He's wearing his usual apron, and it's completely covered in flour, but he still looks handsome in his old-man way.

I haven't been in here since before everything went haywire with Willa Moon, and I'm happy to see him standing behind the counter. He doesn't say much, but even though he's quiet, he reminds me of Poppy. The same dark skin, the same crinkles around the eyes, the same deep radio-announcer voice. On days when I miss Poppy the most, being around Mr. Walker helps me feel like he isn't so far away.

Mr. Walker reaches out his arms, and I practically fall into them. I squeeze him probably a little too tight before letting go.

"Exciting week, huh?" he asks.

He raises his bushy gray eyebrows extra high. I know Mom has been updating him, especially since she had to take some time off work, and he's had to handle things pretty much by himself.

"Ugh, that's the understatement of the century, Mr. Walker." I thunk my head down on the glass even though I know that means I'm gonna have to spray it with the glass cleaner and wipe it down before I go. Mr. Walker is very particular about good presentation. "Everybody thinks I'm a liar."

"Well." He taps a gloved finger against his lips. "Did you lie?"

My head snaps up, and I try to get him to see in my eyes that I'm not faking it. I need him to know that I didn't lie, that it was all real. I don't know why, but it's suddenly more important to me than anything else that Mr. Walker of all people believes me.

"No!"

"Okay, then, Ellie-girl." Mr. Walker smiles softly. "That's all there is to it."

I feel like a balloon that just got popped, all the air rushes out of me so fast. I didn't realize how badly I just needed someone to believe me, to trust what I say without my having to explain every little detail to them. Mr. Walker leans an elbow against the glass display case and looks me over for a second. Then he nods once, slowly, like he's made a decision.

"You know…" Mr. Walker's voice sounds scratchy and out of practice, but it makes me feel the way a blanket fresh from the dryer does. "The last time we had an earthquake in Plainsboro, me and your granddad had just got back from our first tour."

Mr. Walker never talks about his time in the army, not like Poppy used to. Poppy had all sorts of stories about how they would flirt with the army nurses and play pranks on each other in the barracks and gamble away their snacks during card games. He always made it sound kind of like summer camp, just a little more gross because of the weather and sharing rooms with so many other guys. Poppy was good at that, turning even the most boring memories into something worth laughing about.

But Mr. Walker never smiled during those stories. His eyes would get kind of watery, and he would sneak into the kitchen and pretend to be busy when no one was watching. I didn't know it when I was really little, but I learned eventually that where they went was nothing like summer camp. And a lot of the friends they made never got to come back home. It was scary and dangerous, and when Mom thinks I'm not listening, she calls it "a terrible waste."

If Mr. Walker is bringing it up now, it must be for a good reason.

"There was another earthquake? I didn't know that," I say. "How come Poppy never told me?"

"Ray never did too well with details." Mr. Walker scratches at his forehead with his gloved fingers. He looks around the shop slowly before checking the clock. It's nowhere near closing time, but he walks over to the door, flips the sign to CLOSED, and pulls down the blinds anyway. "Come on." He jerks his head toward the kitchen. "I want you to see somethin'."

I don't spend much time in the kitchen. I got banned in kindergarten—after I thought you could make Play-Doh pie if you threw a ball of the stuff in the fancy food processor (which is honestly a pretty understandable mistake for a six-year-old to make, I think)—so it feels strange to walk past the mixers and tray racks and all the big containers of shortening and flour as we make our way to the back office. It's full of papers and boxes, but it's really tidy. All the papers are stacked evenly, and the carpet looks like it's been vacuumed today.

"Will you hand me that trash bin over here?" he asks.

He sits down at his desk with a loud *oof* sound. Standing up and sitting down is getting harder for him and his old bones every year, he claims.

When I turn around and set the small metal bin down on the desk, I almost gasp. "Where are your gloves?"

I've never seen Mr. Walker's hands before and looking at them now is kind of like seeing a moose in person. You know they exist, but putting eyes on one is so rare and strange that it's hard to believe it even when you see it. His hands are wrinkly, and his fingers are long and slim. But other than that, there's nothing remarkable about them.

He smiles and it shows off his one gold tooth. "I take 'em off for special occasions."

"No offense, Mr. Walker, but there's nothing special about today." I plop down in the chair across from him and lean my elbows on the desk. I think about the photographer that I found camping out in the tree in our backyard in a sleeping bag cocoon last night and roll my eyes. "Except that it's another day in a string of terrible days, each more horrible than the other."

"I wouldn't say that."

He tips over the trash can, and a bunch of junk falls out onto the shiny wooden surface. A couple of crumpled receipts, an empty can of Diet Pepsi that I'm pretty sure was my mom's, and a dried-up old strawberry. I try not to call anyone crazy, especially not older people, but this is a little weirder than usual for Mr. Walker. I thought he was gonna tell me some kind of story, not start sorting through his trash. Ugh. Today really is the worst.

I tilt my chair back on two legs in that way my mom is always warning me against. I'm getting ready to say *Thanks but no thanks, I'm not in the mood to play with trash today*, but as soon as I open my mouth, Mr. Walker pushes the shriveled-up strawberry across the desk to me. He barely brushes his fingertip against it, but suddenly, immediately, it changes from a gross brownish black to a bright ruby red. The leaves even extend to full bloom.

"Thunderbolts of Jove!"

I lose my balance and fall back in my seat, landing on the ground in a giant heap of wayward legs and arms. It's not... There's no way!

Mr. Walker is laughing when I finally manage to get myself upright again. I push myself up on my elbows and peek over the edge of the desk. I know what I saw, but I don't believe I saw it. But there, with a big old smile on his face, is Mr. Walker taking a bite out of the strawberry. He raises his bushy eyebrows up and shrugs.

"Surprise."

*

Up is officially down and down is officially up. As if things couldn't get any weirder in my world, Mr. Walker, my poppy's best friend, the semi-silent baker, the Guy with the Gloves, is a superhero. It's too much to process, honestly. And I've gotten pretty good at handling heavy stuff recently, so that's saying a lot.

This is why Mr. Walker's been wearing the gloves my whole life! Everyone thought he was weird, but really he just had hands that could do things no other person could imagine. All this time, he was *magic*.

"I'm gonna be honest, Mr. Walker. I'm freaking out here." I feel like I'm vibrating out of my skin. I stand up and throw my hands in the air. "This means it's genetic! I must have inherited these powers. Everything makes so much more sense now. I can't believe—"

"Ellie-girl, ain't no way it's genetic. We're not related by blood, remember?" He kind of laughs as he says it and I deflate a little.

Oh yeah. Good point.

"I still haven't ever wrapped my head around it," he says, shrugging. "Best I can figure, it was the earthquake from back in the day. One of those once-in-a-lifetime—or twice-in-a-lifetime—things that's rare enough to change everything, down to our very being. Who knows why it shook some powers into us, but here we are."

I flip the seat back upright and sit down. I have so many questions, my brain feels like it's running lap after lap around the track and each one produces another rapid-fire hypothesis.

Mr. Walker seems totally content not saying anything more until I do, so I decide to start with the basics.

"Why didn't you say anything earlier? I could have used a Professor Xavier a week ago, before my whole life got flushed down the toilet."

I cross my arms over my chest. I don't want to be mad at Mr. Walker, I really don't, but how could he leave me to figure out everything on my own like that? I thought I was a freak of nature, an anomaly, some monster. If I'd only known that there was someone out there like me—someone I loved, even—I wouldn't have felt so alone. Because that's the worst part about being different. The loneliness. It's hard to think of yourself as the same as the person next to you when it seems like no one else is anything like you.

I'm excited and sad at the same time. Finally, I don't have to wonder if there's something wrong with me—if these powers are some kind of curse on me and me alone. But if Mr. Walker has had them this whole time and I didn't even know, I must have been doing a way worse job at managing mine than I thought.

Mr. Walker's smile gets a little smaller then, and I can't help but feel bad. I didn't mean to upset him. It's just a lot. All of this.

"When your granddad passed, you know the last thing he said to me?"

I shake my head.

"He said, 'Don't let my girls get lost.' I didn't...I didn't know how to help you." He huffs. "To be honest, I thought getting all my mess mixed up in you and your mama's was just gonna make it worse. But I realize now that was just me being a coward."

He taps the table while he stops to think. Mr. Walker never got married or had any kids, and now that I think of it, he never had any friends I knew outside of Poppy and my mom. I wonder if maybe he's been alone because of his powers.

"Am I..." I don't want to say it, but I can't hold the thought in my head for another second. "Am I gonna be by myself, you know, because of..."

I hold my hands up, and he shakes his head.

"It's not... These powers ain't what you think. They're not a death sentence. They're not the end of the world." He frowns and keeps going. "For a long time, I thought they were. I was terrified. Of myself. Of what I'd seen overseas. And then I got *these* and it just felt like nothing would ever make sense again." He holds up his hands in front of his face and looks at them like he's never seen them before. "And I just shut down. Closed myself off from the world."

He presses both hands down on the desktop.

"I've had these powers for fifty years, and I still don't completely understand them. Heck, I've spent half of that time hating myself for not somehow getting them a few years earlier.

Before the war. I could have saved so many people. Could have changed so much." He frowns. "I don't know what I would have done without your granddad. Probably would have lost my mind trying to get rid of them."

I sit up straighter. "Can you? Can I?"

"No can do, kiddo." My heart cracks open in my chest. If Mr. Walker hasn't figured this out yet, then there's definitely no hope for me. I'm a mess. "But I reckon we can learn how to use 'em the right way," he says. "And maybe we can even help some folks with 'em. Together."

Together. That sounds so much better than what I was doing before, hiding from my powers and also hiding them from everyone else. Mom always says two heads are better than one, and I guess figuring out how to use your superpowers with your seventy-year-old adopted grandpa is as good a place as any to put that theory to the test.

Poppy had a lot of sayings, like "She was madder than a wet hen" to talk about Gramma Candy's temper, and "If the creek don't rise" when he hoped something would happen but didn't want to make any promises just in case something went wrong. But his favorite was "The only way out is through."

It was his motto. And he said it was true of every single superhero story. You didn't win a fight by running away from it. You won by dealing with the things that scare you the most head-on. If either of us is gonna get to the other side of this, we're just gonna have to face it.

I look down at the gloves Mr. Walker always wears and cock my head to the side.

"Mr. Walker?"

"Yes?"

"You know you don't have to wear the gloves, right?" I ask.

At first he looks confused, but then his bushy eyebrows wrinkle together and he looks scared instead.

"No, no. I . . . I can't take 'em off. My hands got too much power. They're too unpredictable." He shakes his head. "It's safer this way. Better if I just—"

I hold out my hand. He doesn't take it. He looks at it like it's an old-timey bully threatening to steal his lunch money. I know why now—he wore gloves because he didn't want to expose his secret to anyone, but also because he thought he was dangerous.

But I don't take my hand back. This can be our first lesson together.

"No, really! I've learned some stuff already." I hold my hand up even higher. "You gotta trust me, okay? I promise it's safe."

Mr. Walker hasn't let his hands touch another person's skin for longer than I've been alive because he was scared of what might happen if he did. I can't even imagine how lonely that must have been, being scared of your own body while everyone in town looked at you like you're crazy. But he doesn't have to be lonely anymore. Neither of us does.

"I promise," I say again. "It's safe."

Mr. Walker closes his eyes, and like not knowing if your

parachute is gonna open but leaping from a plane anyway, he grips my palm and gives it a firm squeeze.

His eyes shoot open when nothing happens and start to well up with tears. There's a quick buzz of electricity that goes from his hand to mine and then back again, just like when I revive something that makes me gasp.

"That's never happened before!" I shout. I'm so excited I could burst. We're already discovering cool new stuff together. "It must be because we're the same!"

Now that we're in this together, I immediately start asking him all kinds of questions. Like is there a way to get around the whole killing-one-thing-to-bring-something-else-back-to-life issue? And if touching something once brings it to life, does another touch kill it again? And what's the deal with the super-hearing and super-smell? Can we get rid of those? Wait! Do they make him a better baker? I bet they do because—

It isn't until he cuts me off that I realize I've been spilling all my questions out loud like an overflowing watering can.

"Ellie?"

I take a deep breath. Whoa, I'm tired. Finally having a Professor X to guide you through your superpowers requires a lot more question-asking energy than I thought it would.

"Um, yes?"

"We'll figure it all out." He ruffles the hair on top of my head. "Let's take it one day at a time, huh?"

I nod.

"Yeah," I say. "That sounds good."

I smile. I'm already thinking of the Saturday-morning tutoring sessions we're gonna have, and the amazing stuff we're gonna unlock about our gifts, and all the spectacular things we can do in this simple, sleepy little town together. The earthquake and the disaster on TV wasn't the end like I might have thought.

This is just the beginning.

"You know the only way out?" I ask.

He nods. Over his shoulder, I can see the framed photo of him and Poppy in high school, sitting on the hood of a beat-up old car, smiling at the camera. I guess Poppy's still helping us figure out what we're doing, even now.

Mr. Walker puffs out a heavy breath and wraps his arms around my body. I drop my face onto his stomach and squeeze him back extra hard, so he knows I understand.

The only way out?

Through.

People always say to pick yourself up and dust yourself off

but I don't think that saying counts when you've been covered in dirt from head to toe for days. Well, not actual dirt. More like emotional dirt. But whatever, according to Mom, dust or no dust, there's no excuse to become a seventh-grade dropout. So I try to channel all the confidence that Mr. Walker has in me, all the love that my mom has for me, and march through the front doors of the school with my head held high.

Mom gave me two whole days after the Willa Moon accident to lick my wounds before she sat on my bed and ran a hand over my head. I'd been hiding under the blankets for what I'm sure was a world record of twelve hours before she forced me to sit up and face the music. She was gonna take one more day off work at the bakery to sort things out around the house, but I needed to get back to class. No more relying on Bree's trusty homework delivery service.

I've never missed hiding under my blankets more than I do right now, though.

I walk straight back to my seat in Language Arts and try to ignore the way Marley and her sidekick, Jules, stare at me the entire way. I know Marley has never been my biggest fan—she's always thought I was weird because I like "babyish" stuff like comic books and fantasy worlds instead of makeup and YouTube makeup gurus—but the way she stares at me now takes the evil eye to a whole new level. This is the I-wish-I-could-turn-you-into-goo-and-flush-you-down-the-toilet eye.

I know what everyone thinks about me. It's not just the news and internet. Even though my episode will never air, I can hear every conversation in every corner, and a bunch of them are about me. About how Abby never should have been friends with a freak like me anyway. Or about how I tried to use Martian's death to get Willa to pay me to bring him back, how *I* asked *her* for money. Some people are mean about it, saying stuff about me and my mom. They've heard doctors on the radio asking questions about where my dad is and making assumptions about my home life, and it's just . . . It's a lot.

Even the kids in my science class, who saw the frog thing with their own eyes, are calling me a liar and a scammer in the hallways. But even after this whole mess, I'm still stuck with these powers.

It's weird. I didn't want anybody to know about my powers—did so much just to try and keep it a secret—but it got out anyway. And I thought that would be the worst part. But you know what's worse than everyone knowing about what I can do? Everyone thinking I was faking it all along.

I know who I am, and what I am, but the rest of the world thinks it was all for attention. And yeah, I don't want all that pressure on me to be and do what everyone expects, but part of me feels really frustrated that this huge part of my life just got brushed aside, dismissed, all because someone else said it was untrue. And it all happened so fast. One day, everyone wanted a piece of me, and now? Now I'm like the gum stuck to the bottom of a shoe—an inconvenience at best.

It makes my stomach hurt to think about, but I'm glad to be away from Mom for a while. The guilt of knowing she lost all her tutoring jobs and now doesn't know how she's gonna make ends meet was starting to eat away at me every time I looked at her. Especially since I can't do anything to risk exposing my powers again now that people have left us alone. So I'm just...stuck.

I sit down in my usual seat next to Bree, and she pushes her glasses up the bridge of her nose.

Her voice is barely a whisper when she leans in close to me.

"You shouldn't listen to them," she says. "Everyone is just jealous."

I mumble back, "You have to say that because you're my friend."

"It's *because* I'm your friend that I know." Her voice is soft and wobbly, like she's unsure. "We are, right? Friends?"

I realize I hadn't said as much yet, but of course we are. It's not like it was when me and Abby became friends—some fast and furious mashing together of personalities and being neighbors and stuff. It was quieter, slower, but that doesn't make it any less real. Watching *Wonder Woman 1984* on the floor together on the eve of the worst day ever definitely solidifies a friendship. It's weird, thinking about someone other than Abby as a real, honest-to-goodness friend, but I like it. I like it a lot.

I smile and nod. "Obviously."

She only smiles a little, but it's more than usual, so I know she's really happy.

When Mrs. Harlow comes in and clears her throat, the first thing she does is start talking about the group project we have to do on *The Giver* before fall break. It's one of those junior-high assignments that sound big and important but is really just a fancier way of presenting our information than the perfectly good tri-fold posters we used to make for science fairs in elementary school.

"Mrs. Harlow?" Marley's hand shoots up, but she doesn't

wait to be called on before she starts talking. "Are we going to be able to choose our own groups for the project?"

She glances over at Sammy Spencer and winks—actually *winks!*—at him. I practically shiver, it's such a scary sight. Marley pretty much drools all over her desk anytime he does anything in class, even if it's something as small as a sneeze. I wouldn't be surprised if she's already come up with a recipe for how to cook and devour him like a steak dinner.

Sammy raises his hand before Mrs. Harlow answers. It takes a lot of energy for me not to roll my eyes out of habit the second he starts talking. Every time Sammy does, well, anything, I think of the way Abby's eyes used to go all wide and goo-goo ga-ga when Sammy's name came up in conversation. My whole world may have fallen apart, but one thing is still true: Sammy Spencer and his blue-eyed, button-nosed self is a major pain in the butt.

Mrs. Harlow calls on him and smiles extra bright since he's such a Goody Two-shoes.

"Do we, um, have to work in groups?" he asks. He rubs at his elbow through his green-and-white baseball tee. "Could we choose to do it alone?"

Mrs. Harlow says no, but she looks sorry about it before starting her lesson. Since Bree brought me my homework while I was out, when Mrs. Harlow starts talking about verb tense, I'm not completely lost. The sound of Bree's pencil scratching as she writes down the vocab words for our next quiz is a little distracting, but I notice that it's not overwhelming like it was before. I can even tune out some of the whispers between Marley and Jules when they start gossiping about who Sammy will ask to the Halloween dance, even though it's weeks away.

I settle a little easier into my seat as I focus on the board.

*

We might as well be studying crickets, the science room is so quiet when I walk in. It feels like that nightmare where you're in front of a crowd in nothing but your underwear, only having your superpowers exposed during a frog dissection is way worse than accidentally flashing your tighty-whities, I'd say.

I don't know if everyone still hasn't recovered from being at the scene of the crime during the dissection the other day, but the whole class pretends not to look at me when I find my seat, and they definitely don't speak to me. Overnight I went from being the most talked-about person in the world to not even being able to borrow a pencil from one of my classmates. But honestly, I can't figure out which is better.

When I sit down at my lab table, Mrs. Morales is still out in the hall yelling at people to stop running or holding hands. I pull out my textbook and turn to the page from the homework Bree brought over and pretend to read. If my nose is buried in my book, I can at least *act* like I don't care about being a semi-friendless loser.

I pretend so well I almost forget that my lab partner is Sammy Spencer. If I didn't think it would attract so much attention, I would slam my head down onto the page.

"Um, hey, Ellie," he says.

I close my eyes for a second and brace myself. Here it comes, another person to make me feel bad about the accident. If people knew how hard it is to keep earth-shattering powers to yourself, I bet they'd be a little more sympathetic about things! I mean seriously, who among us *wouldn't* accidentally bring a frog back to life during science class under the circumstances? No one, that's who!

But that doesn't matter. Because Sammy is one of them—like the Marleys and now the Abbys of the school, all shiny and perfect—and that means he doesn't care about how embarrassed I was or how horrible it is to feel like everyone hates you for something you can't control.

"Just say it." I open one eye and look at him. I've never been punched before, but this moment feels like I imagine it would if I were in a boxing ring waiting for the first hit. "Let's get it out of the way. Call me a freak. A weirdo. Tell me you don't want me to sit anywhere near you."

I sigh. I'm suddenly really tired. I just wanna go home. I wanna hide in my room again and cry so quietly my mom can't hear me and try to fix what's wrong.

Sammy jerks back and looks all shocked. His cheeks are red, even.

"No, I wasn't— I wouldn't..." He stares down at the table for a second. "I just wanted to see if you were okay? It was pretty intense, um, after everything."

Huh? Why would Sammy care about that? About me?

I shrug. I don't know if he's serious or not. Regardless, I don't feel like being the butt of another joke.

"How come you didn't do any interviews?" I ask him. "You were right there." I look down at my homework and trace over the letters of my name just to have something to do with my hands. "For a front-row-seat exclusive, you probably could have gotten, like, a hundred new followers at least."

"I don't really care about followers and stuff." I can sense him shake his head. "Besides, I know how it feels to have a bunch of people looking at you when don't want them to. Feeling like they only pay attention to you for one thing. Yeah, um. It sucks."

That surprises me. Sammy is the king of attention. All the girls love him, and all the boys want to be him. But now I remember his face when Marley shoved her camera at him during class, how pink his cheeks got when she called him cute. Or how in Language Arts he asked if we really had to do the projects in groups instead of just being able to do them alone. And it makes a little more sense. Maybe Sammy does get it, at least a tiny bit. Having people looking at you and fawning all over you can be the worst, especially when it's for all the wrong reasons.

"You're smart," I blurt out. I want to smack myself in the head the second I say it. *Real smooth, Ellie.* "I mean, um, you always have the answers and stuff. In Advanced Language Arts."

I want to tell him that I kind of understand all the hype. That he's cute in that your-curly-hair-and-pink-cheeks-make-you-look-like-a-tall baby-if-babies-could-read-*The-Giver*-and-understand-themes-and-stuff kind of way, but he's not just cute. He's also nice, and he volunteered to do the grosser parts of the dissection without so much as a complaint just because I made up a story about my ethics and whatever. And he did it even though I wasn't all that nice to him.

Sammy smiles, and it's a big, real one. The kind you do only when you mean it.

Just then the bell rings, and everyone settles into their seats. Mrs. Morales starts her lecture at the front of the class about photosynthesis.

Sammy writes on the notebook he's supposed to be taking notes with and slides it toward me.

YOU AND YOUR FRIEND WITH THE GLASSES ARE THE SMART ONES. Lol. I'M JUST TRYING TO KEEP UP.

He has that squiggly-scratchy handwriting most boys have, but I'm able to decode it. And when I do, I let myself smile without thinking about how he must be a secret jerk just because Abby and Marley have some big, ridiculous crushes on him.

Bree's a genius. She's like a real life Shuri.

I almost feel embarrassed for bringing comics into it before I remember that Sammy spends his free time at Wrigley's, too. He doesn't hesitate before he writes back.

MARVEL OR DC? WARNING: IF YOU SAY DC, WE CAN'T BE FRIENDS ANYMORE.

I feel a laugh bubble up inside me, but I don't let it out. Oh my gosh. Sammy Spencer is a *nerd*. And he just called us friends.

It's not a big deal, I know it isn't. But it feels like a big deal, seeing the word *friend* on the paper like that next to something about comic books. Before the powers, I didn't really have friends—not like a lot of people do. Pals you can have sleepovers with and invite over for dinner and go to the mall with. I never really needed anyone other than Abby. But now everything feels different. Like, I don't know, making one person your home is a bad idea because there's nowhere to run when it falls apart.

I tell Sammy I'm DC based on the coolness of Wonder Woman and Nubia alone, and we should just call it quits now. And then he says something about the Avengers' superior strength, and I tell him he needs to read the old stuff because obviously the movies have taught him nothing, and before I know it, I've missed most of Mrs. Morales's lesson.

Today, with all the eyes on me as I walked through the hallways and all the whispers in class, it felt like my skin was too small for my body and it would never fit right again. But it's getting a little bit easier with every minute that ticks by. Every silly joke Sammy writes and every snippy reply I make back helps erase that feeling. It reminds me of watching *WW84* with Bree, and dancing in the kitchen with Poppy and my mom back in the old days. Easy. Fun. No pressure.

Sammy is probably just being nice. I know that. We're not besties just because of one class where we passed notes. But . . . for the first time in a long time—maybe ever—I feel like it wouldn't be so bad to open up my world a little. It's scary to think about, that after all this time being one way, I'll have to learn how to be another, but maybe it's time. Maybe I can be my own home and invite other people into it.

Bree. Sammy, even.

By the time the bell rings, we've filled up the entire page, and Sammy is still laughing at my comparing Falcon to a beef-jerky stick wearing a jet pack. I barely even notice the stink eye Marley shoots in my direction on her way out the door.

"Hey." Sammy shoves his books back into his backpack. "In Language Arts, we have that project. And I don't really— Well, do you think— I mean, it might be fun if, um, you and Bree and me made a group." His dimples get all dimply as he smiles. He shrugs. "I think we're the only ones who actually read the book over the summer and care about the assignment. And I'm not so great at public speaking, but you are. So."

Open up my world. Be my own home. Invite other people in.

"Yeah," I say. "That would be really great."

27

Everyone is staring at me

and my stomach flips with nervousness at being back in the cafeteria. I've only been out for a few days, but it feels like a whole lifetime. But the faster I get back into the groove, the faster things can go back to normal. Or as close to normal as possible, I guess.

I remind myself that being surrounded by people is better than being trapped in my room, which has felt more like a dungeon than my castle lately. I missed being in the world. But more than anything, I missed Abby.

I spot her sitting with Marley and the other cheerleading girls, and it's the first time I've seen her in person since that night in her room. Her hair is still up in the same high ponytail all the cheerleaders wear, even on days when they don't have practice or even a game to cheer at. I guess they all like to look the same, so there's no question about whether they're all one big blob of pep and school spirit.

Their table is right in the middle of everything, like they're the sun and everyone else is orbiting around them. Some people gawk at the table like every single one of them is Ariana Grande times one hundred. If Abby wanted to Make Her Mark, then this is as good a way as any to do it, I guess. She definitely has people's attention.

I try to ignore the nauseated feeling at the thought that a few weeks ago, me and Abby were ... not a blob exactly, but at least a puddle of similarity. We brought the same chocolate-chip granola bars to eat for breakfast in the car on the way to school, laughed at the same goofy jokes, watched every Willa Moon movie the day it came out (which I've sworn off of for the rest of my life, thank you very much). But it was other stuff, too, that marked us as two halves of the same whole, stuff no one would ever see.

Like the way my heart beat faster whenever she was around. The way my palms got all clammy. The way I sometimes smiled at her and didn't even realize I was doing it.

I shake my head and grab my tray a little tighter. *That's over, Ellie. Get a grip.*

The sight of Abby sitting with the cheer girls looking like she's having the time of her life vacuums all my hope that things could go back to normal right out of my brain. Nothing about this is normal. Normal would be me sitting with my best friend and the two of us fading into the background together. Not her sitting with the most popular girls in school and me being able to hear Ginny Freeman whisper to Autumn Boland: "I heard Ellie's mom is gonna move them to Idaho to join the witness protection program because she's so embarrassed."

Now I just want to get through this lunch period, this day, this school year, as fast as humanly possible.

Bree waves to me from her seat at a round table against the far side of the cafeteria, and I walk in her direction a little faster. I know it's not gonna do any good, but I hope that maybe if I move faster and sit quieter and shrink myself smaller and smaller, maybe no one will notice me. No drama, no more weird nicknames. I've had more than enough attention to last me the rest of my life.

I sit down across from Bree and crunch down on a celery stick. Ew. Even the taste of one of my favorite vegetables makes me sad since I have to eat it in the same room as my former best friend. It's a fact of life: Everything is made a million times worse when you're already bummed out.

At the center of the room, the cheerleading table erupts with loud, cackling laughter, and Marley looks over her shoulder at me. I don't need super-hearing to know who the butt of that joke was. Bree reaches over to my tray and swaps my dish of celery for her small bowl of grapes.

She dips a piece of celery in some ranch dressing and crunches down like it's a Snickers bar or something. For some reason, trading food without even bothering to ask reminds me that I have someone who's looking out for me. I'm not alone. My whole body feels a little looser, like maybe things aren't completely horrible. She pushes her glasses up her nose and gets real serious.

"Okay, tell me the truth," she says. "Was *The Ribbit* right about Willa? Does she really smell like pond water and old newspaper?"

My laugh jumps out without my permission. Pond water? Where do people get this stuff?

Me and Bree get so caught up in how we think celebrities smell (Bree thinks Harry Styles smells like stale bread, and I think Taylor Swift smells like the oak trees on Main in the fall right before the leaves change) and the homework I missed while I was out that I don't even notice when the rest of the cafeteria goes quiet. Not until Bree shuts her mouth so fast I can hear her teeth click together, and her face gets that look on it like a skunk is raising its tail in her direction.

"Back in school, huh, *freak*?"

Marley pulls her pink-and-white tote bag higher on her shoulder. None of the cheer girls carry backpacks. Like the high ponytails, the bag is part of the unofficial-official uniform.

I look around and all eyes in the cafeteria are pointed at us. The room smells like the hot casserole they served for the main course today, but it sounds the way it does right before a tornado. Everything completely settled but promising something big and terrible to come sooner than you think. I can't decide whether Marley is the tornado or the aftermath yet, but I don't really wanna stick around to find out.

I push my chair back, grab my backpack under my chair, and pick up my tray. I say a silent prayer to every single member of the Justice League. *Please let me get out of here. Please let me get out of here. Please let me get out of here.*

"Where do you think you're going?" Marley steps in front of me and crosses her arms.

Good-for-nothing Justice League. That's why I've always secretly rooted for the Avengers. Ugh.

"You owe me an apology," says Marley.

She points a finger in my face, and it feels like everyone must have practiced their loud *Ooooooo* sound while I was out. It's so perfect it might as well be in three-part harmony.

I roll my shoulders back like I'm not afraid.

"I don't know what I would say sorry to you for."

I move the tray a little so it makes enough distance between us that I can duck out of the way of another pointy finger. I know I shouldn't, but when Marley rolls her eyes, I check out the cheer table over her shoulder, hoping to see Abby looking back at me.

Abby, who kicked Greg Hoffman in the kneecap in second grade when he knocked my issue of *The Fantastic Four* to the ground on purpose. Abby, who once glued Miranda Feinstein to her seat in music class when she said I couldn't find a note if it was on fire. Abby, who never backed down from anybody, especially when they were being mean to me. There's gotta be some piece of my old best friend in there. There just has to be.

But when Abby finally stops staring at her tray, she looks right at Marley, and when one of her new friends—a girl I don't know but recognize from gym class—starts laughing, Abby doesn't say anything. She doesn't move a muscle. She looks like a statue. I feel like I'm on a roller coaster that only drops down, down, down, and my throat gets tight like I want to cry. But I won't. I refuse to.

All this time I've been trying to shrink my powers, hide them, to make my world as simple as possible. I've been holding on to my friendship with Abby even though Abby wants stuff that I can't, and don't want, to give her anymore. No matter how small I try to make myself, or how comfortable I've been in the shadows all my life, there's no going back to the way things were before. And maybe that's a good thing.

"You should say sorry because you made me look like an idiot, pulling that prank during the dissection for attention. Now Willa Moon thinks I'm some kind of liar." Marley stops and taps her lips. "Hmm, but on the bright side, at least I'm not a loser. Like *you*."

It's like a scene in a movie. One of those horrible ones where you don't know whether to laugh at or cry for the main character. Only this isn't fake. This is my real life. And everyone around me is laughing and I can see my old best friend with her new friends pretending like she never met me and I can hear the boys at the table behind me saying it's what I deserve.

I stare at Marley as she holds her hand up for a high five from one of the cheerleader girls who moved to stand beside her. And for the first time ever, instead of seeing a shiny, perfect girl who can't be touched by the rest of us mere mortals, I see someone who really, really wants to be liked. And someone who says terrible things to people because she thinks that's the way to do it. Marley isn't perfect, at all. Or untouchable. She's just another seventh grader. A mean one.

My first thought is to find my inner Nubia and do whatever she would do. But then I realize I don't have to follow Nubia's strong and powerful lead anymore. I can be—no, I *am*—strong and powerful, too.

And maybe I always was.

I feel the familiar buzzing in my hands that starts in my fingertips and runs up my arms and through my entire body that always happens right before I use my powers. There's nothing here to resurrect, but there is something I can save: myself. I've met one of the most famous people in the world, I've brought dead things back to life, I've been a good person with a big heart even when people weren't kind to me and my best friend traded me in for high ponytails and big bullies.

I did all of that. Me. Elliot Leigh Engle. I've faced Big Bads bigger and badder than Marley Keilor and made it to the other side. I can do it again.

"Maybe I am a loser, Marley," I say. "But you know what I'm not? Someone who needs to push other people around to feel better about myself."

I set my tray back down on the table and try to ignore how fast my heart is pounding. I know every eye in the cafeteria is on us, but I can't stop. I might not be cut out to be the kind of superhero Wonder Woman is, who runs directly into danger with a shield and a uniform and near-limitless strength. But I can be a different kind of hero. A quieter kind. The Ellie Engle kind.

"I may be a freak, but at least I'm not the villain in everyone else's story."

Light *ooh*s and *ahh*s start up around us, and Marley's face gets redder and redder. She clenches her fists at her sides and opens her mouth like she's about to really let me have it. But before she gets the chance, all the eyes in the cafeteria turn to Sammy Spencer, who's climbed up on top of his chair. He clears his throat.

"If Ellie is a freak, then so am I," he shouts. His cheeks are pink like they get sometimes when he's embarrassed, but he doesn't stop. "I'm proud to be a freak!"

"Sammy, oh my gosh, what are you doing!" Marley shrieks. "You're gonna take her side?"

Sammy ignores Marley and offers me a small wave. Sammy

is the most popular boy in our grade, and he's defending *me*? My eyes dart around the cafeteria, and all of a sudden, people look a little less sure about whose side they're on. I don't expect anyone else to join Sammy to support me, but then to my right, I see Bree climbing up on her chair as well.

Bree, who barely talks to anyone besides me, and always in an almost-whisper, yells, "I'm a freak, too!"

My throat starts to get all tight again like I might cry. My smile grows so fast it almost hurts my face. I think of the Justice League and the Avengers and the Fantastic Four as I look between them. Maybe only one of us has superpowers, but we're definitely a team now. No doubt about it. If this is the kind of battle I have to fight, I'm lucky that they're the ones ready to stand beside me.

Suddenly, Ms. Winston, who was supposed to be on lunch duty, rushes into the room. Her hair is flying all over the place, and she has a piece of lettuce stuck to her cheek.

"Sammy and Breonna, get down from there!" she shouts. She slaps a hand on her forehead and mumbles, "A woman can't even eat her mixed greens anymore without everything going belly-up."

Sammy and Bree look a little caught out, but they both jump down. We better not push it any further, either, because Ms. Winston looks like she's swallowed a frog, she's so panicky and frazzled. Teachers stepping in always manage to make bad situations worse somehow. It's, like, science. Marley looks even more furious now that Sammy and Bree have made their declarations, and Ms. Winston is moving in our direction, her long, flowy skirt waving behind her like a flag. We don't have much time before she drags us both down to the office. I can't read minds, but I know what Marley is thinking.

"You don't get the last word, weirdo!"

Marley lowers her voice so much it sounds like a snake hissing when she takes a step toward me. She reaches for the open carton of milk sitting on my tray, lightning-fast, and before I can jump back to avoid getting splashed with the contents of the carton, a flash of pink and brown leaps in front of me. I close my eyes to brace for impact as Marley lets go of the carton. But when I open them, instead of it hitting me, I see Abby, furious and soaked in lukewarm chocolate milk.

Ms. Winston reaches us just as Marley gasps and the carton lands on the shiny lunchroom floors with a dull thud. Since I'm in the splash zone, some leftover milk drips onto my sneakers.

"Ms. Winston, I didn't mean to—"

"That's enough, Marley," she snaps. I've never heard Ms. Winston sound so serious before. "You're coming with me to the principal."

Ms. Winston examines me and Abby, still standing in the middle of the floor with twin looks of shock and grossed-outness, and shakes her head sadly.

"You two head on down to the nurse for a change of clothes, okay?"

I turn to leave, but Ms. Winston places a hand on my shoulder to stop me. When I turn to look at her, she flashes me a quick wink and mouths: *Welcome back, Frog Girl*. I can't help but smile. Coming from Ms. Winston, the name sounds more like a compliment than anything I've ever heard. She hardens her expression fast when she turns back to Marley, though.

"Those crocodile tears don't impress me, Marley." She points at the door. "Let's go."

I cover my mouth to keep a laugh from escaping.

Nothing tastes sweeter than justice. Well, except maybe the chocolate milk that's currently soaking my sneakers, I guess. But still.

Me and Abby walk most of the way to the nurse's office in silence. When the joy of watching Marley get in trouble fades, I have no idea what to say. I'm mostly just confused. Why would Abby jump in front of me if we're not even friends anymore? Doesn't she know siding with me in that cafeteria means that Marley is gonna make being on the cheerleading team extra hard for her? It doesn't make any sense. All Abby's wanted since the first day of school was to make her mark. And she wanted it so bad that when it was me in the spotlight instead of her, she didn't even want to be around me anymore. So why would she take a flying carton of milk to the chest for me?

Abby stops suddenly a few feet from the nurse's door. Inside, some kid is snoring while Nurse Lee plays *Word Scrambler* on her phone. I'm pretty sure she thinks the sound on her phone is muted, but I can hear the little beeps and chimes every time she gets a word right clear as day.

"Ellie..." Abby frowns down at her sandals. "I feel really bad."

"Yeah, I bet. You're never gonna get this milk stain out of that fabric."

"Not about that!" Abby's head jerks up. "I mean, okay, yes, a little about that. But mostly about everything else. I never should have left you when you needed me. It was stupid."

She reaches up and pulls the ribbon out of her hair that's been keeping her cheerleading ponytail in place. When she shakes her head, her hair falls down onto her shoulders in waves.

"I thought Marley was the person I needed to be like if I wanted to have an impact, but I was wrong." Her eyes are wide and sad as she adds, "I'm really sorry."

My emotions are like a tornado, swirling around inside of me and knocking everything off-balance. I'm sad and happy and confused and mad all at the same time. My stupid heart wants to accept Abby's apology right away. This is all I've wanted to hear since that night in her room when she basically said she didn't want to be friends anymore.

Abby has always wanted Big Things. She's always wanted to Make Her Mark. And always, even now—maybe especially now—the only thing I've ever wanted was for things to be normal. Simple. I just wanted to be around her, and for my mom to be less stressed all the time, and to disappear into the big, complicated worlds of Gotham and Metropolis and Central City when the real world got to be too much. And I'm okay with that. I'm learning that I have to be, because if I leave how I feel about myself up to other people, I'm always gonna feel horrible.

And the way Abby has treated me lately hasn't been the way a best friend is supposed to act. She turned her back on me when I needed her because who I am made her uncomfortable. And that's not fair. I love her a lot, so much it used to hurt sometimes, but I don't love her more than I love me.

"So, can we go back to being friends again?" she asks.

I swallow down a lump in my throat that feels like a baseball has lodged itself against my esophagus. I try to think of what my mom would want me to say, and then I think of how my poppy would have handled this, and then I imagine how Wonder Woman would respond. But in the end, all I can do is respond the best way I know how. And that's with the truth.

"Thanks for apologizing," I say. "But, Abby. You hurt me. Like, a *lot*. And I don't think I ever would have done to you what you did to me."

Marley said such mean things about me to the news reporters, and Abby didn't even tell her to stop. She just kept hanging out with her. I can't just let that go.

"You've always been so good about not caring what people think!" Abby says, her voice all high and stressed like she gets when her siblings won't listen to her or when she can't understand a math problem. Her eyes start tearing up, and I'm afraid mine might, too. "I'm not like that. But I know Marley was wrong. And so was I."

Poppy used to say that the bad guys aren't all so bad, and the good guys aren't all so good, and that's what makes stories interesting. That there is always some room for change. I know Abby isn't all bad because I've seen her be the funny, fierce, encouraging version of herself for a long time. What I didn't understand before, though, was that Abby isn't all good, either. Just like some of my favorite comic books, she's got some pages ripped at the edges and folded down at the corners. But just because she isn't perfect doesn't mean that I can't love her. And just because she's made some mistakes doesn't mean I can't forgive her.

But that doesn't mean I have to do it right now. I can take my time.

Slowly, I raise my arms, and Abby rushes into them to squeeze me in a mega-hug.

"It's gonna take a while for me to forgive you, I think," I say when we finally separate. "But I still love you."

Maybe not the heart-fluttery, stomach-flipping kind of love I had before, but something different. Maybe even something better.

Abby nods and wipes at her runny nose with the back of her hand. She doesn't add "Forever and two days" like we normally would. And even though it makes my heart hurt just a bit to know that things have already changed enough that all we can promise each other is that we'll try to be better tomorrow than we were today, I think that's okay. Because if being a hero is about learning to adapt to new, and sometimes scary, circumstances over and over again, then maybe that's what a friendship is, too. Maybe all we ever needed was to take it one day, and one challenge, at a time.

28

Mr. Walker is definitely not
Professor Charles Xavier

and I'm no star pupil, that's for sure. He's super patient with
me while we work on mastering my powers using the skills he's
stored up over the past fifty years, but he's pretty bad at explaining where I'm going wrong. There have been a lot of raised
eyebrows (him), rolled eyes (me), and pained grunts (both of
us, thanks to my terrible hand-eye coordination) already this
morning—and it's not even noon.

I tell him that weekends are supposed to be for sleeping in
and eating cold pizza for breakfast in your pajamas, not this
supernatural Saturday school, but he doesn't seem to agree.
Instead, Mr. Walker is trying to teach me how to reverse a

resurrection. He says it's not a skill I'll need often, but I should know how to do it just in case. But he didn't warn me that it'd be so much harder than going the other way.

"Ellie-girl, focus now, come on," Mr. Walker says, nudging the small potted cactus across the desk toward me. "Remember what we talked about. It's not about pushing outward, it's about..."

"Inviting in," I say.

He's said the same thing to me so many times I'm pretty sure I'll be reciting it in my sleep tonight. I wouldn't be surprised if there were just cacti in their little pots, tap-dancing over my head like pint-sized Broadway stars when I close my eyes.

I mumble, "Whatever that means."

He doesn't even try to hide his smirk.

"You know I got the same super-ears you've got, right?"

"Oh yeah." My cheeks get warm when I remember that just like me, not too much is getting past Mr. Walker anymore. Oops. "Good point."

I don't waste any more time. I tap the tip of the cactus again, just like I did ten minutes ago when I revived it the first time. But just like the last twenty times in a row, nothing happens. My theory is Mr. Walker just wants to torture me with useless skills because he enjoys seeing me suffer, but I'm waiting for more evidence to back up my claim.

I flop back into my chair.

"I'm never gonna get it." I'm all sweaty and my hands feel like shriveled-up raisins from how much I've had to use them today. I cover my face and groan. "What's the point, anyway? We don't *want* stuff to die, right? Bringing things back to life is the whole point of the power!"

Mr. Walker shakes his head gently. His hands don't have gloves on them anymore, so when he flips them over so I can see his palms, I trace the wrinkled lines and scars with my eyes. He closes his hands into fists and then opens them back up slowly, like he's releasing a butterfly into the air.

"A lot of people got hands that can take, but not a lot of people got hands that can give. You can do both. You gotta understand how one isn't possible without the other."

He breathes out extra slow the way he always does when he's thinking one of his heavy thoughts. The kind that a few weeks ago he wouldn't have shared with me, but now he shares all the time. Since he told me about his powers, I learn something new from him every day. Sometimes—during our lessons like today—it's about how to be a better super. Other times, when we don't feel up to working, he just slides me a cupcake and we talk.

Well, mostly I talk, but sometimes he chimes in. He has so many memories I can't believe I'd never heard about. Funny stuff like the time him and Poppy got chased out of the movies for not paying when they were fifteen, or the date when he went to kiss his girlfriend and accidentally spilled a banana split down her shirt. And sometimes it's not so funny. Sometimes it's about losing his friends to time as they all grew up and grew old, or about the terrible things he saw during the war.

But each day makes me feel even closer to him, and some-how, also closer to Poppy. This is one of those moments where I can almost imagine Poppy being in the room, his loud voice telling both of us to stop being so sappy and get back to work.

"Don't let them hands go to waste, Ellie-girl," Mr. Walker says, voice low and encouraging. "You gotta know all the ways you're extraordinary—and really know them good—'cause people are gone try to make you forget."

I nod. Mr. Walker has this way of making me feel big, even when I'm having a hard time figuring something out.

Okay. Okay, slow and focused. Just like he taught you.

I close my eyes and channel all my energy into my hands. Instead of focusing on radiating the energy out like I do when I bring something back to life, when I place my finger on top of the cactus, I think about absorbing the energy. Like tak-ing a deep breath in, my body feels like it expands a little, like there's a balloon in my stomach that gets bigger for a second just before disappearing completely. And when I open my eyes, the cactus is deflated and flopped over the side of the pot, just like it was before I brought it back to life. Meanwhile the droopy sunflower in his window perks back up to its full height.

"Mr. Walker, I did it! It's dead! I killed it!"

I jump up from my seat, and so does he. I start doing a

disco move that I remember Poppy doing once upon a time while Mr. Walker pushes his arms out and back and around in a circle like he's doing a malfunctioning running man. We're both laughing and smiling, and I never thought I would be so happy to kill something, but I guess in this case, it's a good thing.

"Of course you could do it!" He beams. "When you know how to control your powers..."

"They don't control you." I finish our motto for every lesson, and Mr. Walker high-fives me.

It's a lesson we're both still trying to learn, not being afraid of what we can do. Instead, embracing it and all the cool and sometimes scary stuff that comes along with it. I glance at the clock over his shoulder to check the time. Mom wants me home so we can have lunch together, since she's been on the hunt for a new job all week and we haven't seen each other much.

"Gotta go, Mr. Walker. I'll see you after school on Monday?"

"I'll have one of the new lemon swirl cupcakes waiting for you."

I call out my good-bye as I jog out the door and hop on my bike. I can't help smiling all the way home.

29

Mom looks like a supervillain

stressed out over an experiment gone wrong when I walk into
the kitchen a little after midnight. I yawn and scrub at my
eyes to see her more clearly. Her hair is falling out of her usual
pineapple, and her foot is tapping hard against the stool she's
sitting on. Like always, she has a big book open in front of her,
and I can tell from where I'm standing that it's her budget book.
She'll spend hours and hours trying to force the numbers to
make sense, but they always end up the same way. Not enough
to go around.

We spent all afternoon together, watching TV and eating
snacks. I know it was her way of making up for lost time this
week, but it's hard to enjoy those fun moments sometimes,

because they're always gonna be just moments. We can't make up the time we spend apart because we're always losing time. She's gotta work hard to support us, and now I'm working extra hard with Mr. Walker to get my powers under control so that I can help support her. I don't know how I'm gonna do it yet, but I do know it's gonna take a lot of time. And it definitely won't have anything to do with millionaire pop stars and their yippy little dogs.

Or, well, *dog*. Singular.

I feel silly standing here with sleep-crust in my eyes, wearing my comfy oversized Black Lightning T-shirt and fraying bunny slippers while my mom looks the opposite of cozy. I woke up and wanted some water, but now my mouth is dry for a whole different reason than stinky sleep-breath. Part of me wants to turn and walk back upstairs. There's so much that my mom needs that I can't give her, and so much she's lost all because of me.

"Ellie!" She grabs her chest when she spots me trying to tiptoe out of the room. "You surprised me, girlie. I gotta get you a bell to wear or something, let me know you're coming."

She laughs but I don't feel too peppy, so I just shrug.

"Hey, Mom."

She smiles like I've just handed her a bouquet of roses as big as my head as I come closer. She's happy to see me even though we were together for most of the day. I feel like I have a gumball trapped in my throat.

"You should be asleep, Belly." She holds her arms out for a hug, and I walk right into them. I breathe in deep and smell her cocoa-butter-and-Ivory-soap scent.

"What're you doing up, huh?" She pulls back and kisses me on the forehead. "I've been reading up, and apparently super-hero mothers have a legal obligation to make sure their children get a full eight hours every night. It's required for you to be in peak world-changing condition."

When I don't respond right away, she takes a long, hard look at my face. She must not like what she sees there, because she slides off her stool and crouches down to reach inside the cabinet with all the Tupperware containers. When she stands back up, she has our old Bluetooth speaker in her hands, lighting up and coming to life. She blows on the top of it, and some dust billows onto the counter. She clicks around on her phone a little bit before setting it down and turning to me with a smile.

"What are you doing?" I ask, confused. She starts step-touching and snapping her fingers with a gleeful grin on her face. Music begins playing, and she clicks the volume up louder and louder until I have to raise my voice so she can hear me over it. "Do you know what time it is?"

I should have guessed that my mom officially losing her marbles would be on the schedule this week. Master a new super-skill, and a few hours later, your mom starts randomly doing the running man in the middle of the night. It's just my luck.

"You're doing too much talking!" she answers, using her socks to do a full Jackson 5 spin on the slick floor. "You used to love this song, remember?"

I wasn't really paying attention before, but when she says that, a familiar sound of horns blares out into the kitchen. All of a sudden, it's Saturday morning and Poppy is coming down the stairs pointing at the two of us and hitting a spin move that he always said his hips were too old for. I don't have any powers to learn or understand or worry about. There's no stack of bills on the counter. There's just the sound of Maurice White singing about remembering the twenty-first night of September.

"I think we're long overdue for a dance party, don't you?" she shouts. She grabs my hand and spins me into a dramatic dip before wiggling her shoulders with the beat. She's a little out of practice, just like me, but she always gets into the groove quick. "Come on, Ellie-Belly, get *down* with your bad self!"

"Mom..." I shake my head and my smile drops. This is silly. Why are we dancing when we haven't solved any of our problems? She's still stressed about bills. We still don't know what we're gonna do to make up for her tutoring jobs. I'm making some progress on better understanding my powers with Mr. Walker already, but there's still a lot I don't know. "I'm not a little kid anymore. You don't have to try and distract me with stuff like this."

She frowns and turns down the volume but doesn't stop the music entirely. She just cups my cheeks in both hands and smiles down at me. I feel small, but not in a bad way. Like her steady hands are enough to keep me together even though I kind of feel like a vase that someone knocked off a table that shattered all over the floor right now. Just a bunch of pieces, waiting to be picked up.

"You know it's not your job to worry about all this, right? You've got enough to think about in that big brain of yours without concerning yourself with boring grown-up stuff like bills."

But that's the thing. Maybe bills are for grown-ups, but that doesn't mean they don't have anything to do with me. Mom wouldn't have lost her jobs if I'd been more careful about revealing my powers. Dad is off in Arizona living his fancy new life to go along with his fancy job, but I'm still here. Aside from Mr. Walker, we're all each other has now.

"If I don't look out for you, who will?" I ask. "You love baking more than anything, and you barely even get to do it anymore because of money stuff. And I try not to complain, but I miss you all the time because you're gone so much, but it's still not enough."

"Oh, my baby." She sighs. "Have you been holding this in all along?"

I nod. My lip starts wobbling and I can't keep in my tears. I tuck my face against my mom's shoulder and neck, and her arms wrap around me so tight I lose my breath. It's been ages since I cried in front of her, since I just let myself feel grade-A horrible, but I give in this time. I just let myself cry and let her rub my back.

"I miss you, too, Belly. All the time. You're the best, most special thing that ever happened to me. You know that, right?"

I shrug. I haven't really thought about it like that.

"I'm sorry, sweetheart. Let's make each other a promise right now, huh?" She puts her hands on my shoulders and pushes me back. Her voice is tight, but her eyes are soft. "You'll stop trying to hide all these big feelings from me, and I'm gonna make some changes to my schedule so I can be around more. I think we both need each other more than we were letting on."

People always talk about weight being lifted off them, but I just thought it was a figure of speech. But as I make this promise, it feels like I've had a thousand-pound elephant on my back for more years than I can count, and he just finally let go. I can breathe a little better. It's too hard trying to be so mature all the time. Like my mom said, I want to try being just a kid for a little while. Even if I *am* a kid with unimaginable untapped power.

"Mom?" I ask.

"Yeah, baby?"

For some reason, I miss Poppy so much it aches right then. I miss his big laugh and his funny stories and the way he used to poke fun at Mr. Walker's baking even though he ate every crumb of every dessert Mr. Walker ever set in front of him. It's more than just wanting things to be simple again, I realize, it's about wanting things to feel *whole* the way they always did when Poppy was around. I want us to laugh together more and be afraid a little less. I thought the way to help my mom was to stay quiet and out of her way, but really, we're meant to take up the same space. And that starts with me not disappearing into my own worlds, alone, when ours starts feeling like too much.

"Tomorrow, do you think you could come with me to Wrigley's?"

It's my favorite place in all of Plainsboro, and I want us to experience it together. Maybe then our worlds won't feel so far away from each other anymore.

My mom cocks her head to the side in surprise but ruffles my hair and agrees without hesitating.

"Of course I'll come with you!" she says. "I need some more reference texts anyway. You think they have Frog Mama manuals? Or, wait! Frog Mama*nuals*—get it? You see what I did there?"

I roll my eyes as she laughs at her own joke, and I reach for the speaker. The song has changed from "September" to "Boogie Wonderland," and I hold out a hand just as the chorus starts to play. She takes it and squeezes so tight I don't think we'll ever let go.

In all the comics I've read, in between the heroes' bouts of saving the world, I don't remember Wonder Woman ever dancing in the kitchen with her mom, or Superman laughing so hard that his ribs began to hurt because he tried to do the splits and couldn't get up again the way I'm doing right now.

But then again, I'm not all that interested in saving the world. I'm pretty busy trying to just save myself. And I never needed to be a superhero to do that.

I just needed to be me.

30

Mom is a mother hen

when Sammy and Bree show up to work on our project the next day. She's really strict about making sure we're good hosts, so she's trying to do a quick clean of all the newspapers and random coupon envelopes that have collected on the table and countertops this week while she was out job-hunting. She rushes around while Bree and Sammy sit at the kitchen table, the rubric for our project and their books and notebooks spread out in front of them.

"Belly, grab these two something to drink from the fridge, will you?" my mom calls out as she passes me with a stack of junk mail piled high in her arms. "And take Mr. Burt upstairs! I don't want it to look like we're running a pet store in our kitchen."

Burt the Betta Fish, I correct her, but only in my brain. I sigh. At least she added the *Mr.* to his name as a sign of respect. I rush him back upstairs to his place on top of my bookshelf, where I keep my all-time most favorite comic books. I know he can't read them, but I like to believe my favorite heroes are looking after him when I can't.

When I get back downstairs, Sammy and Bree look a little surprised by all the activity, but they both smile anyway. They're just good like that. Always willing to sign on for whatever craziness comes along with the Engles.

I slide them some cans of Yoo-hoo across the table and sit down. I expect it to feel weird having them both in my house while my mom freaks out about how clean our kitchen looks, but it doesn't. I guess that's a side effect of having your entire life rearranged by necromancy and a world-famous pop star. Stuff like getting caught having messy countertops and inviting more than one guest over at a time for the first time ever starts to feel less like a crisis and more like just another Sunday.

When Mom's finally satisfied with the state of the kitchen, she presses a quick kiss to my cheek and heads toward the stairs.

"I'll be in my room if you need me, okay? Don't resurrect, retool, or revive any living things while I'm gone. Love you, Ribbit!"

I groan at her momliness and the new nickname, but Sammy and Bree just laugh.

"Don't encourage her!"

Bree snorts. "I like it. Ribbit has a ring to it."

"Yeah, better than Frog Girl, for sure," Sammy adds as his pink cheeks somehow get even pinker.

"Besides," Bree adds, "it's good that your mom can make jokes about it. My dad is too serious. He definitely wouldn't be as cool about things as your mom has been."

Bree's nose is buried in her copy of *The Giver*, even though I know she's not reading it. I'm learning that sometimes Bree finds her way to books when she wants to disappear. Some people have security blankets; Bree has security books.

"Your dad is pretty tough on you?" Sammy asks, and scratches his elbow nervously. That's the kind of thing that Marley and the other people who have crushes on him probably don't see. He does a lot of stuff nervously. Turns his baseball cap from the back to the front and then back again. Scratches his elbow. Bounces his knee.

"Yeah, but all professors seem kind of boring and serious. So I think it's just part of the job." Bree shrugs. "Even though I'm his daughter, he treats me like a student. Everything has to be A-plus level, down to how I wash the dishes."

"I would fail the chores class," I say, trying to lighten the mood. "I'd definitely get an F in doing the dishes."

"But you could get extra credit for taking care of the lawn, since you can bring stuff back to life!" Sammy smiles. "I'd get a solid F-minus in laundry. My moms say they haven't seen my bedroom floor since I was old enough to walk."

We all laugh as Sammy tells a story about being six and his laundry hamper collapsing on top of him. He says it took him five minutes to swim his way out, and by the time he reached the surface, his moms were both just standing there, cracking up. He even imitates himself as a little kid by lying on the floor on his back, wiggling his arms and legs around like an upside-down turtle.

For a while, we spend our time talking about our embarrassing memories, and even though it's not a competition, the Frog Girl story would definitely get the gold medal. But still, we laugh until our stomachs hurt, drink Yoo-hoo until we burp, and talk until our voices get tired. We only work on the project for a little while, but it doesn't take long to decide what we're gonna do.

The Giver is about a world without pain, hunger, or suffering, and a community of people who don't have to hold on to any bad memories. But there's a boy named Jonas who knows everything about the past and wants to tell the people he loves that life is bigger than the boring gray lives they've been given. There are good things and terrible things and beautiful things and ugly things. And all of it comes together to make a fuller world.

So Bree suggests we break the class into groups and then pass out cards with different moments in history on them.

Some of the cards will have things about the past that people would probably rather forget, but for each card, we all have to come up with three reasons why it's important that we never stop talking about it.

We come up with our list of historical moments and decide to meet in the school library tomorrow during lunch. I can't remember the last time I was actually excited for the bell to ring for lunch, since it usually just means lukewarm green beans and bland pizza, but I can't wait for tomorrow. I always thought Abigail Ortega was the only friend I needed. And when she didn't want to be friends with me anymore, I worried that was the end. I'd just be stuck by myself.

But Bree and Sammy showed up for me when everything was in disaster mode, and they just keep showing up. I feel like I'm in *The Grinch*. Not that my heart was ever as cold as the Grinch's or anything, but it's definitely growing a couple sizes after spending time with them. A group hug is a little too sappy for the moment, but I make a mental note to hug it out later. It's the natural order of things.

"I know we're done with our homework, but..." Sammy takes off his Dodgers cap to shake out his curls before putting it back on. "Do you guys maybe wanna keep hanging out?"

Sammy wants to keep hanging out! Bree's smile is so wide it shows off all her teeth, and I know I probably have the same grin on my face. My body buzzes with the kind of warm feeling I haven't felt in a long time. That the-Grinch-heart-growing feeling. It's like my brain almost forgot what it was like to make new friends, but my heart remembered.

"The new Doctor Strange movie just dropped," I say. "We could watch that?"

Bree snaps her fingers like she's got a great idea. "I'll get the popcorn!"

She doesn't wait for Sammy to say yes—she just hops up and walks to the cabinet that I got the popcorn out of when we watched *WW84* together. She moves like she knows her way around the kitchen already. Sammy stands up and starts shoving his school stuff into his backpack. For a second, I think he might have changed his mind or something and decided to go, but then he zips up his backpack and says, "I'll grab the drinks!"

He pulls the last three cans of Yoo-hoo out of the fridge, walks into the living room, and plops down on the carpet in front of the TV. The doorbell rings while Bree gets the bowl for the popcorn, so I shout, "Don't forget to add extra butter!" while I jog to answer it.

I don't even notice I'm smiling until I open the door, and my face goes from happy to confused. Abby is standing on the porch in one of her old Rising Phoenix gymnastics T-shirts, holding an issue of *Nubia and the Amazons*. Her brown eyes focus on what's happening behind me before either of us says anything, and I know she must be a little lost. It's not every day I have friends over who aren't her.

It's not every day I have friends who aren't her at all, I guess.

"Hey," I say.

"Hi." She smiles a little and holds up *Nubia*. "I went to Wrigley's on my way home from the gym earlier. I thought maybe we could, um, read it together?"

Abby never reads comic books, and she definitely doesn't go into Wrigley's unless I drag her there. It feels like she's trying to make a truce, and I can't help but feel lighter. Since me and Abby made up outside the nurse's office, we still haven't really gotten back to normal. Or not exactly normal, but at least back to the way it was before . . . everything.

Seeing her on my doorstep with a comic book with my favorite character of all time is something bigger than I have words for.

"What were you doing at the gym?" I ask.

"Trying to see if I can get back on the team." Her voice is kind of quiet. "Turns out, maybe cheerleading wasn't for me."

"I thought you didn't want to do gymnastics anymore, though?"

"I missed it, I guess." She hugs the issue of *Nubia* to her chest. She cuts her eyes to Sammy and Bree behind me, talking excitedly about something. "I've been missing a lot of stuff lately."

I take in a big gulp of air. "Do you . . . want to come in?"

Her eyes lock on mine and for a second, it's just like it used to be. My heart flips, and my stomach feels like it's full of hopping crickets, and my face gets warm. But then Sammy says, "Hey, Ellie! The popcorn's getting cold!" and everything comes rushing back to me like a bucket of cold water over my head.

A lot has happened in such a short time. Both of us have changed so much, it's almost unbelievable that the faces that look back at us in the mirror in the morning are the same as they were a few weeks ago. But if training with Mr. Walker has taught me anything, it's that you're never done learning. About yourself, or about the world. Abby is learning, too, just like me.

We still have a lot of figuring out to do. But...maybe we can do it together.

On one condition.

I look back over my shoulder at where Bree and Sammy are throwing popcorn into each other's mouths. Bree, who is shy around strangers and would rather read books than talk. Sammy, who everyone thinks is cool as a cucumber but gets nervous speaking in front of crowds and watches anime with his mom in his free time. Bree and Sammy, who stood up for me in front of a bully and didn't run away from me when they found out about my powers.

Bree and Sammy, my new friends.

I hold my arm up, blocking the door. Abby may have apologized, but that doesn't mean I can just forget everything that happened.

"Bree and Sammy are really great, and super nice, and they like me even though I have powers," I say.

I've never told Abby no before or that she couldn't come into my house. But this is important to me. I channel the same type of energy that Mr. Walker taught me this morning. I invite in all the positivity and laughter from Bree and Sammy in the living room and use it to make me feel confident. When I feel strong, I roll my shoulders back and make my voice firm.

"Nobody is too cool for anybody else in here. So if you're gonna be rude or make them feel bad, you can leave now. No Marley Keilor clones allowed." I take a deep breath and let it out. "Got it?"

Abby nods her head so fast I'm worried she might get whiplash.

"Yeah! I swear." She holds a pinkie up and I link mine through hers. "Besides, I read comic books now. And I threw away all my magazines with Willa Moon on the cover. She's *so* last week." She smiles that smile that makes the entire room feel like it's full of sunshine. "I'm officially ready to join the club."

"What club?" I ask.

Abby makes a face like I'm the most ridiculous person she's ever met. "Um, the Magnificent Four. Duh."

"The *Fantastic* Four, oh my gosh." I laugh as I step to the side to let Abby in.

She kicks her shoes off, marches straight into the living room, and jumps into the popcorn-throwing contest with Bree and Sammy like we've all been friends forever. The sound of my friends laughing rises to meet me as I shut the door. When

I lean against it, a smile practically splits my face. This is the same thing me and Abby have done a million times before—leave our shoes by the door and grab our snacks to camp out in the living room for a movie—but somehow, today, it couldn't feel more different.

This time, it feels like the beginning of something extraordinary.

AUTHOR'S NOTE

Once upon a time, my mom transformed the wall paint in my bedroom from a standard eggshell to a bright canary yellow. My little sister and I relished the freedom that those four sunshine-drenched walls immediately granted us. Everything was bigger, grander, somehow in our new room—us, our stories, our dreams. We were Michelin star chefs in a Parisian restaurant. We were haute couture designers crafting looks for our Barbie Fashion Week show. And for one brief but spectacular moment in time, we were even the long-lost Black Olsen siblings.

Within the walls of my childhood bedroom, my sister and I made all manner of dreams real (except the Olsen sibling thing—those hopes were dashed pretty quickly, I'm afraid). Our mom encouraged us to pursue every passion, explore any fantasy we could conjure up. For a time, we were given the space to be *wondrous*. Now that yellow room represents the ineffable magic that's reserved only for our safest, most trusted spaces.

Because one day we outgrew the room, and our mother's loving home, and we stepped into a world where Black girls who will one day become Black women are encouraged to shrink ourselves. There are reminders everywhere, all the time, that Black girls should make ourselves smaller, more palatable. And if we're not careful, we can begin to believe them.

Ellie Engle Saves Herself is a book about a young, queer, Black girl who believes herself to be unspectacular—who has been convinced that she's safest in the shadows. Ellie isn't alone in this. This very moment, all over the country, queer and trans children, especially those of color, are being reminded with every book banned and every anti-LGBTQIA+ law passed that there are people out there who wish them small. Wish them invisible. My hope is that this story (in addition to providing the kind of laughter that makes you pee your pants a little) will serve as a declaration that no one can take away our right to exist without fear or shame. No one.

Ellie Engle Saves Herself is the sometimes-silly, always-joyous reminder that wonder, that *magic*, aren't things we outgrow—they're in our very bones. It's a reminder that not all heroes wear capes. That sometimes they're our teachers, or librarians, or nurses and paramedics. Sometimes they're authors and booksellers and editors. Sometimes they're folks who thought about giving up but decided to fight another day.

And sometimes, no matter what the world says, our hero is the person looking back at us in the mirror.

In community, with love,

ACKNOWLEDGMENTS

When I began writing *Ellie* in the spring of 2021, I was worn thin by a global pandemic, and by the powerlessness that so often accompanies the inability to protect the people you love from harm in any significant and tangible way. Around this time, we were also at the beginning of a wave of book bannings and challenges around the country that would, inevitably, include my queer Black YA novels. As I watched people I love suffer from a rampant virus that the United States refused to take meaningful steps to curb, and the very children I write for denied access to stories that affirmed their experiences, I needed to believe in magic.

I needed to believe in the ineffable, the wondrous, and in a world where young Black folks feel empowered to take control of their own lives and step into their limitless power—without regard for what the world may have to say about it. And thus, the nerdy, big-hearted, baby gay necromancer Ellie Engle was born.

Ellie's story wouldn't have been possible without the immediate enthusiasm and advocacy of my incredible agent, Patrice Caldwell, who took a fever dream of a proposal and helped me fashion it into my first middle grade novel. I'm stunned, constantly, by the overwhelming support of Disney Hyperion and all the folks behind the scenes who have gone above and beyond to put this story out in the world: Ashley I. Fields, Kieran Viola, Guy Cunningham, Sara Liebling, Jerry Gonzalez, Matt Schweitzer, Holly Nagel, Danielle DiMartino, Maureen Graham, Jess Brigman, Monique Diman, Lia Murphy, Vicky Korlishin, Loren Godfrey, Michael Freeman, Dina Sherman, Maddie Hughes, Bekka Mills, Crystal McCoy, Tyler Nevins, and the ever-brilliant cover artist Mirelle Ortega.

Plainsboro-sized thanks are due to my editors, the legendary Steph Lurie and the inimitable Rebecca Kuss. It was their brilliant editorial guidance that shaped this book into something I will forever be wildly proud to have created.

I owe so many of my peers a debt of gratitude for having work that keeps me reaching towards greater honesty, sharper craft, and, of course, funnier fart jokes. But I want to especially thank Erin Entrada Kelly, Kyle Lukoff, Kwame Mbalia, Julie

Murphy, and Kacen Callender for being early readers of the book and providing such generous blurbs (I'm still not sure I've fully recovered from them). To justin for inspiring me to push myself past my comfort zone as a writer and to venture into the fantastical; to Rosie for answering every frantic call and every celebratory text; to Vanessa and Arri and Chann and Reece for the support, the memes, and the laughs (okay, okay, and the occasional tears).

Thank you to the New Leaf team: Meredith Barnes, Hilary Pecheone, Eileen Lalley, Pouya Shahbazian, Katherine Curtis, Veronica Grijalva, and Victoria Hendersen for being the well-oiled machine that makes dreams come true. To Kate Sullivan, for your insightful feedback; and Trinica Sampson for, well, literally everything—you deserve a Nobel.

Thank you to my family, but especially my mother, who has never once stopped fighting for me. I hope you know I'm fighting for you too.

Thank you to the superheroes in disguise as booksellers and teachers and librarians and bloggers and advocates and defenders of diverse voices. I am here—we're all here—because you refused to give up on these stories. And finally, thanks to you, dear reader. Whether you've donned your cape already or haven't quite pinned down your superpower yet, you are filled with magic. The world, *my* world, is better because you're here.

If you didn't know that before, I hope you do now.